Chief Sunrise, John McGraw, and Me

Chief Sunrise, John McGraw, and Me

Timothy Tocher

Cricket Books
Chicago

Text copyright © 2004 by Timothy Tocher

Illustration copyright © 2004 by Greg Copeland

All rights reserved

Printed in the United States of America

Designed by Anthony Jacobson

Fifth printing, 2006

Library of Congress Cataloging-in-Publication Data

Tocher, Timothy.
 Chief Sunrise, John McGraw, and me / Timothy Tocher.—1st ed.
  p. cm.
 Summary: In 1919, fifteen-year-old Hank escapes an abusive father and goes looking for a chance to become a baseball player, accompanied by a man who calls himself Chief Sunrise and claims to be a full-blooded Seminole.
 ISBN 0-8126-2711-3
 [1. Baseball—Fiction. 2. Runaways—Fiction. 3. Race relations—Fiction. 4. United States—Social life and customs—1918–1945—Fiction.] 1. Title.
 PZ7.T5637Ch 2004
 [Fic]—dc22

       2003023407

For Judy

All Aboard
April 4, 1919

S itting by a campfire is one of those things that sounds a lot better than it is in real life. At least that's my experience. I was huddled so close to the flames that April night that the smoke was burning my eyes, yet I was still chilled. That fire drew all the dampness of the Georgia winter out of the ground, and it was crawling into my bones to hide.

My old man had left me here, about a stone's throw from the railroad tracks. He was out scouting the town. We had arrived in the morning, jumping off a freight car while the engine was stopped at the station a quarter mile or so ahead. We laid up in the brush all day sleeping. By dark, my stomach was flat empty. I knew better than to say anything. The old man is testy enough when his belly's full. But my stomach wouldn't shut up.

At last he said, "Start a fire. I'll be back with something that will shut off that growling. Anybody comes nosing around, our name is Burns, and we're looking for work."

Three steps, and he had faded into the shadows.

My name's Hank by the way. Just Hank. The old man has used so many last names that I wouldn't know my real one if I heard it. He was Henry Banks once for a whole season when he played third base for Iowa in the Prairie League. But by September he was drinking up the paychecks as fast as they came in. Soon he was out of the lineup, and a week later off the team. Anyway, that was the longest we ever kept a name. Most times we change every month or so.

The old man had been gone long enough for the fire to burn low twice. I threw on more wood, then unbuttoned my shirt and pulled out my mitt. It was the one thing I owned other than the clothes on my back. I didn't have a baseball, so I used a smooth, round rock to form the pocket.

I pulled the mitt onto my left hand and gripped that rock in my right. Staring into the fire, I saw old Ty Cobb step into the batter's box. He crouched and sneered at me.

"Whatta ya got, Busher?" Ty scoffed.

"Try this on for size," I mouthed and went into my windup.

Before Ty Cobb could swing, I heard someone crashing through the woods. I knew the drill. I stuffed rock and glove into my shirt. While my fingers were fastening buttons, my feet were kicking dirt on the fire. When the old man burst into the clearing, he pointed up the tracks, and I took off running. My legs were stiff, but the angry shouts behind us were enough to get the blood flowing. I set my gaze on the back of the old man's neck and kept moving.

We were running alongside the railroad tracks, and the voices were drowned out by the shriek of a train whistle. The engine's headlight swept around a curve and lit us up like we were posing for a picture. I heard a loud crack—rifle fire. That's when I knew that the old man must have done more than steal a chicken. My heart raced, and my legs picked up the pace.

"They're shooting in the air. Keep moving!" the old man called over his shoulder.

The old man's stride is a lot longer than mine, but I was gaining on him. Whether it was the booze he's sucked down through the years, or the fact that he'd been running longer than me, I caught him up.

"Hop in that car," he shouted.

I looked at the train, which was roaring alongside us now. There was a boxcar whose door was open partway. As it drew closer I leaped. My hands grabbed the bottom of the door where it met the floor. My feet scrabbled wildly, and for a moment, I thought I'd slip off. Then I got one knee up to the floor and pulled myself into the car.

I crawled a few feet and lay gasping for breath. I heard a thud as the old man's hands grabbed the door. I turned my head, and our eyes met. He looked like his body was one big hurt, and I pictured his legs scrabbling for a grip like mine had.

I crawled toward him to grab an arm and help him in. Then I stopped. The moon lit things up, and I could see his eyes threatening punishment if I didn't haul his sorry butt into the car. But I stayed where I was. He gave one last shuddering heave, which almost got a leg up. Then he lost his grip and was gone.

The whistle screamed, and I felt the jolt as we picked up speed. The engine was through the crossing and ready to roll. My side ached, and my arms stung from the scrapes and scratches I had picked up running through the woods and climbing into this boxcar. I knew I'd feel hungry again as soon as I got my breath back. But I had to smile. I was fifteen years old, and I'd finally gotten away from my father.

I sighed and crawled over to the boxcar door. I planned to slide it closed if I could, to shut out the cold night air and to keep it from drawing the attention of any other bums who might be looking for a ride. But first I stuck my head out into the draft and let the wind whip my hair. I was free. Whoever had been chasing the old man would keep him busy long enough for me to disappear.

I knew what I wanted to do—find a town with a ball club and get a tryout. I might be small for my age, but put me at shortstop, and I'd show anyone I was a ballplayer. Baseball talent was the one good thing I'd inherited from the old man.

I breathed a last gulp of that springtime air and forced the door along its rusty track.

"Best leave it open, son," said a voice from a corner of the car. "It's dark enough in here already."

My instinct was to jump. If there's a worse feeling than a strange voice from the darkness when you think you're alone, I hope I never find out. My heart was half-way off the train, but my brain stopped me in time. We were in open country now, roaring down a grade, and if I didn't kill myself, I'd be bound to break something. Besides, there weren't enough miles between me and the old man yet. After what I'd done, I had to avoid him for the rest of my natural life.

I turned and barked in my gruffest voice, "Show yourself, man," while my fingers fumbled with my shirt buttons. I pulled out the rock, my mitt falling to the floor, and cocked my throwing arm, ready to let fly into that dark corner.

"Easy there," came the voice. "If you're fixin' to throw somethin', at least let me get my mitt on."

That stopped me. I kept my arm cocked, but didn't fire the rock as he stepped out into the moonlight. He was taller than the old man, at least six feet. His arms were long, hanging down past his knees as he shuffled forward. He wore overalls, scuffed boots, and a ragged-looking mitt. He took the mitt off, stuck it under his left arm, and offered me his hand.

"Chief Sunrise, the greatest Indian to ever step on a baseball diamond, pitching immortal in the making," he said.

I lowered my arm, but held on to the rock. More than once I'd seen the old man offer to shake just so he could get ahold of somebody. I took a step to the side so I was farther away from the open doorway and still out of reach.

"Hank Cobb," I answered. "Stay back or you'll be meeting the immortals tonight."

He chuckled, but stopped where he was. "Did you say Cobb?" he asked. "Any relation to Ty Cobb?"

"Only in talent, far as I know. Folks say I play baseball a lot like he does."

Actually, no one had ever said that. The old man had put me to work selling peanuts at a ballpark in Atlanta a couple of years ago. I saw the Georgia Peach play in an exhibition game, and I'd been modeling myself after him ever since. I figured it was a safe name to use as the old man had never given us that one.

"Then you must cut a mean figure on the playin' field," Chief Sunrise said. He lurched toward me, causing me to jump back, but it was just the motion of the train throwing him off balance. I took another step away from that yawning door.

"Where you headin'?" I asked.

"Gainesville, Florida," he answered. "The New York Giants are in spring trainin' there. I aim to show Mr. John McGraw what I can do. Talk him into takin' me north with the team."

"You must have some arm," I said.

I was thinking that he was crazy. John McGraw had been in the big time for thirty years as player and manager. He must have seen a thousand bushers with big dreams. I can't imagine that many of them ended up with the Giants.

"Wait till this train gets to Gainesville, and you'll see," he promised.

We were quiet for a minute, then Chief said, "Was that the law tryin' to get in this car? If the police are goin' to stop the train, I'm gettin' off now."

I looked at the floor. "The law's not after me."

This seemed to satisfy him because his next question was, "You got anythin' to eat?"

I shook my head no and slid to the floor. If he was going to hurt me, he'd have done it by now, and I didn't have anything worth stealing. Besides, if he could meet McGraw, why couldn't I? I didn't expect to sign with the Giants, but it would be a thrill to watch a big-league team in training.

Chief Sunrise settled down, too. He curled up in his corner, using his baseball glove as a pillow. In a few minutes, he was snoring. I crawled into the opposite corner, slid my glove under my head, and tried to shut out the noise of the train and let its motion rock me to sleep. We were going to arrive hungry and filthy. There was no sense in being tired, too.

No Gain in Gainesville

My dreams were filled with the old man's eyes. He hung in the doorway of the boxcar, still as death, his pupils bright pinpoints in the moonlight. They say a snake can paralyze a mouse, freeze it in its tracks by staring at it. That's how I felt in the dream. I wanted to crawl back into the car, but I couldn't move. Then the old man's hand grabbed my foot. That broke the spell. I kicked out and scrambled to my feet.

It was Chief Sunrise. He had nudged my foot with his to wake me up.

"Train's slowin' down," he said. "I'm jumpin' off before we get to the station. I can't show McGraw my stuff if I'm in jail."

I was trying to shake off the dream and remember where I was.

"You comin' or hidin' out on board?" Chief asked. "Train goes all the way to Miami if you stay on long enough."

"I wouldn't mind meeting McGraw myself," I said, "and seeing if you can really throw the ball."

Chief waved for me to follow. We stood in the doorway as the train slowed. The whistle sounded, telling us that the engine was approaching the station. I leaned out, but all I could see was more track. If there were railroad detectives, they were safely around the next bend.

Chief looked like an athlete as he leaped from the train. He jumped far out, curled into a ball, and rolled through the bushes that lined the tracks. As soon as I got done admiring his form, I took the plunge. Lord, wouldn't it be great to ride into a town in style someday instead of bouncing alongside the tracks like a sack of mail.

I was still pulling the clinkers out of my legs when Chief grabbed my arm. "Let's cut through the woods," he said.

We wandered away from the tracks for twenty minutes or more. When we struck a rutted, dirt road, we stepped out of the woods and walked toward town. My stomach was quiet for the moment. I don't think it had the energy to complain.

This was my first good look at Chief. I hadn't been able to see much in that shadowy railroad car, and cutting through the woods, I had had to concentrate on every step to keep from falling or getting lashed with a branch.

I knew he was a tall, lanky man. Now I saw that he had a long face with a square jaw. His straight, black hair hung down in back, and he'd tied it with a piece of string to form a little tail that bounced off his neck with each step. His skin was dark, except for a pink scar that ran down his right cheek. He seemed to have no interest in me, looking straight ahead as we walked.

"What kind of Indian are you?" I asked.

"Seminole—a swamp rat," he said. "What kind of white boy are you?"

That took me aback. "No special kind."

"Where you from?"

Another tough one. The old man roamed around a lot. My mother had died from a fever when I was three, and we'd been on the move ever since. That's how he kept from getting locked up. My past was a blur of drafty rides in boxcars and the backs of trucks. I could remember lots of places, but I couldn't put them in order. So I answered, "Here and there."

This got him to turn toward me and smile. "Let's leave things general for both of us, then."

We rounded a bend, and the rutted track met a smoother, wider road. A weather-beaten truck was chugging toward us, its trailer sagging under a load of scrawny cypress logs. Chief had his thumb out in no time. Filthy and ragged as we were, I was surprised when the truck shuddered to a stop.

"You boys want to earn a dollah?" the driver called.

I jumped onto the running board, imagining the grub I could buy with a buck. But Chief's hand wrapped itself around my shoulder and gently tugged me back to the ground. He leaned into the open window of the truck and asked, "A dollah each?"

"No," said the driver with a frown, "a dollah to split. Y'all are together, ain't yah?"

Chief nodded. "How do we earn that dollah?"

The driver paused long enough to turn his head and spit a long, brown strand of tobacco juice through the open window behind him. Then he turned back to us. "Ride with me to the station and unload this truck."

Chief sighed. "That looks like more than a dollah's worth of work."

The driver shrugged. "Suit yourselves. No shortage of bums hangin' round the station."

The driver ground the gears. Chief hopped onto the running board as the truck groaned and lurched forward, scooping me up in one of his gangly arms to stand beside him.

The driver cackled. "Thought you'd see it my way."

Gainesville was a good-sized town, but it didn't look too prosperous. We rode down streets lined with ramshackle buildings that leaned at odd angles. The bank was brick and there to stay. The others seemed to be waiting for the next hurricane so they would have an excuse to lie down and rest.

When we pulled into the station, there were more beat-up trucks like ours and plenty of equally filthy characters to unload them. Since the soldiers had come home from the big war, there were always more men than jobs. The railroad workers kept their distance as if they were afraid to get their uniforms dirty. But they stayed close enough to yell instructions and to curse when they weren't followed.

Chief boosted me up into the truck, and I started handing down the spindly logs. He carried them to a flatcar, where a railroad man took charge of the actual loading. The hardest part of my job was making sure not to pull out the wrong log. They were tangled together, and whenever I pulled one, three or four others tried to get even by pinning me against the splintery, wooden sides of the truck.

"What use are these things, anyway?" I asked Chief.

"Just keep 'em comin'," he answered, so I figured he didn't know, either.

Twice Chief had to climb up and help me out from under a pile of logs. This made my face burn with embarrassment. Red as I was from the hot sun and hard work, I hoped it didn't show. The old man would have left me to work my own way out. But Chief pulled logs this way and that until I scrambled free. He probably figured the faster we got done, the sooner we would eat.

By the time the truck was empty, two hours had passed, and we were soaked with sweat. Grime from the cypress bark coated our wet skin. Chief's hair had curled up, which made him look comical. He walked over to our employer, who had sat on the running board in the shade cast by his truck, reading a newspaper while we slaved. I walked around the truck so I could approach from the opposite side. The old man had taught me to surround anyone who owed us money.

"You fellahs worked hard," the truckdriver said. "If you're in town next Saturday, I'll be here about the same time."

He handed Chief a silver dollar. My stomach started its growl again.

"Obliged," Chief said, "but we'll be long gone by next Saturday. Maybe all the way to New York."

The trucker spat on his own boot, frowned, and wiped the toe on the back of his overalls. "New York, eh? How you fixin' to get way up there?"

"We're here to see McGraw," Chief boasted. "I can strike out any man wears a uniform."

The trucker laughed so hard, he nearly swallowed his chaw. When he recovered, he rubbed the back of his hand across his watery eyes and said, "You're the living proof of that saying 'a day late and a dollah short,' boys."

He waved the newspaper in our faces. When he held it still, I read the headline: "Giants Bound for Atlanta."

"Their train left yesterday mornin'," he cackled.

Chief didn't say a word. He turned and walked across the street, where what passed for stores in this town were found. I followed. I wasn't letting him out of my sight until I'd eaten my half of that dollar.

Chief walked up to a rain barrel and plunged his head in. He held it under so long that I thought he was trying to drown himself. Then he shot up, shaking the water from his long, black hair like a dog escaping from a bath.

"Wash up, and we'll eat," he said. "If McGraw's gone, we'll follow him."

I dunked my head in the rain barrel, more to cool off

than to get clean. It was going to take more than rain-water to do that job. My scalp had been itching the whole time we worked, and the cold water gave me some relief. We scrubbed our arms and faces as best we could with our bare hands. After a few minutes, we still looked filthy and our clothes still smelled, but a body could tell we had tried to clean up. Judging by the man who had hired us, standards of cleanliness weren't too high in Gainesville, anyway.

My old man would have gone into the general store and come out with a dollar's worth of supplies. Chief walked past it and stopped to wait for me in front of the diner.

The diner's screen door had holes in it big enough to pass your hand through. Yet there were so many flies that they had to wait in line for their turn to zip inside. We sat at a greasy counter where a girl about my age was swatting at the flies with a dishrag. She had bad aim, which worked in our favor, since she used the same rag to wipe off our plates.

We ordered flapjacks and coffee. I won't say those flapjacks were tasty, but my stomach was so glad for company that it wasn't particular. There was a jug of molasses on the counter, and you could help yourself. The tricky part was getting some without flies stuck in it.

It didn't take us long to get outside of those flapjacks. We were sipping our coffee when the screen door banged behind us. In walked our boss from the train station fol-lowed by two guys who looked enough like him to be his cousins.

"Hey, Chief," the truckdriver called, "you're in luck after all. Local boys have a game at the ballpark this afternoon. Maybe the visiting team can use you."

His friends laughed like to split their sides. I figured something was up. But Chief, all he heard was *baseball*. He vaulted off that stool and out the door with me close behind.

We heard the screen door creak, and a voice yelled, "Hotel—ask for Mr. Jameson." Then there were more laughs.

Shortstop
for Hire

I caught up with Chief long enough to ask, "Do you know where the hotel is?"

"Towns like this, it's always on the main street and near the train station. It won't be far."

Chief was right. We hadn't walked more than a block, me struggling to match those long strides of his, when we came to the Gainesville Gables. The hotel didn't look any sturdier than the rest of the buildings on the street. Judging by the few rusty cars and pickup trucks parked out front, it wasn't attracting the cream of society. But it had a porch, and several young women were sitting on it, rocking in its shade. That would have sidetracked my old man, but Chief was all business. He blew by the ladies without a glance and into the lobby. He strode up to the desk.

"What room is Mr. Jameson in?" he asked the man behind the counter.

The clerk's lip curled, and I could tell he was about to say something snotty about how dirty we were, when a newspaper rattled behind us. A voice said, "I'm Jameson. What's your business?"

We turned to see a round, little man seated in one of the worn easy chairs that dotted the lobby. He wore a plaid suit, and his derby was tipped back from his forehead to let the light find the newsprint.

Chief strode over and stood in front of his chair. "Chief Sunrise is my name, and pitchin's my game. I can strike out any man wears a uniform."

Jameson gave a strange sort of smile. "This is why I travel the highways and byways of this fair land of ours— to meet interesting people such as yourself. Who sent you to me?"

"Don't know their names. Boys down at the diner," Chief answered.

"Well, Chief, I'm afraid you're not the right type for my team, which is a shame because I need one more player." Then he looked at me. "Now, the other fellow, he might fit in. Do you play ball, son?"

I didn't miss my cue. Pulling my mitt out of my shirt, I stepped forward. "Hank Cobb. Shortstop's my preference, but I can play wherever I'm needed."

Chief stood with his mouth hanging open. This Mr. Jameson must have an eye for talent, I thought. He doesn't start drooling over size like some so-called experts do.

Jameson heaved himself out of the chair. He pulled a watch from his vest pocket. "What do you say we walk over to the ballpark, Mr. Cobb. We'll see what you look like in front of a few ground balls."

I was at the door so fast that Jameson chuckled. Then I remembered Chief. He was staring at the floor, too dumbstruck to move.

"My guardian has to come, too, sir," I said to Jameson. "He makes all my business decisions for me."

Jameson nodded and said, "Come along, Chief. I may not have a spot for you on my roster, but I'm sure you'll prove useful."

Jameson and I struck out for the ballpark. I looked back to see Chief talking with one of the ladies on the porch. Maybe he wasn't so different from the old man on that count after all. He waved at me to go ahead.

Jameson called out to everyone we met along the way. "Are you coming to the game today? Come see how Gainesville stacks up against my squad," and other such comments.

We rounded a bend, and there it was, Gainesville Park. The Giants themselves had played here just days ago. Burns, Kauff, and Youngs had scooted across the same diamond I'd be on today. The great John McGraw had paced the sidelines yelling advice and making schemes that would carry his boys to the top of the National League in the new season.

Not that it was much to look at. It was one of hundreds of tired, old, wooden ballparks scattered across the South. You could smell the timbers rotting in the humid air.

Come to a game, and you'd better check your seat before you plopped down. Sunny afternoons would cause the tar to drip from the roofing.

Jameson waved to the man on the gate. "There's one more in my party, tall fellow with a scar on his cheek. Don't let anyone else in."

Chief was along in a minute, a half smile on his face. I guessed that he loved baseball as much as I did and couldn't mope in a ballpark. The field was half grass, half hard-baked clay. It was empty except for a thin man who was trying to smooth out the pitcher's mound.

"Pinky," Jameson called, "put down that rake, and grab a bat. This young man claims he's a shortstop."

Pinky ducked into the dugout and came back with a battered baseball and a fungo bat. I was pacing around at short, trying to get a feel for how the ball would bounce on this ground. Chief talked to Jameson for a minute, then jogged out to first base.

I thought I'd have some time to warm up, but Pinky ripped the first ball right at me. I got enough leather on it to slow it down, smothered it with my chest, grabbed it off the ground, and whipped a throw at Chief. The ball flew straight and true and landed in his outstretched mitt with a satisfying smack.

No sooner did Chief lob the ball to Pinky than he blistered another. This time I was ready and snagged it cleanly. Once he saw he couldn't knock the ball through me, Pinky decided to check my range. I spent the next ten minutes scurrying back and forth between second and third. Sweat streamed into my eyes, and my legs ached, but I loved every minute. On the ball field I never felt small, or scared, or confused. I knew what to do and how to do it.

Jameson waved his arms and walked toward Chief at first base. Pinky flipped the bat and ball into the dugout and came out to reclaim his rake. If he'd been impressed with my play, he showed no sign.

I wandered in and found a bucket filled with sun-warmed water. I dumped the first ladle over my head, which was itching like crazy again. The second I drained in one gulp.

Jameson and Chief shook hands and then joined me. I was so excited at the idea of playing for a professional team that I almost burst. But the old man had taught me to hide my feelings, so I tried to look calm.

Jameson said, "Hank, your guardian and I have reached an agreement. Some parts of it you're going to like; some you're not. Are you sure he speaks for you?"

"Do I get to play ball today?" was my only question.

"You do indeed," Jameson said, chuckling. "Chief assures me you're as good at bat as you are in the field. Time is short, so I'll take his word."

"Deal," I said and shook hands with Jameson. Chief had never seen me hit, but I wasn't worried. I knew how to put the bat on the ball.

Jameson walked us back to the hotel. The porch was deserted now, and so was the lobby. We walked past the desk clerk and down a long hallway. I thought we were going to Jameson's room, but when he opened the door at the end of the hall, the room was empty except for a bathtub. Some thin towels rested on one end.

"Shuck off your clothes, and climb in," Jameson said. "By the time you're clean, I'll have your uniform here."

Chief grabbed a bucket and headed to the kitchen for hot water. I turned my back and started peeling off my smelly duds. My undergarments weren't much more than holes, so I was kind of embarrassed. Jameson seemed to understand.

"I supply new drawers and socks," he said. "Your shirt and trousers will be washed."

Chief was back. He dumped the bucket and went for more. Jameson left, carrying my clothes, and I stood in the tub soaking my feet. Three more trips, and there was enough water for me to sit in. It turned black almost immediately, but I hoped the soapsuds would clean me up, anyway.

I had stepped out of the tub and was drying myself on a towel when Chief brought one bucket just for my hair. He mixed a vile-smelling liquid with the water in the bucket and said, "Stick your head in here, and hold it under as long as you can. It will kill those cooties that have you scratchin' so much."

"I think I'll skip that part," I said.

"Jameson says we've both got to go through it or we can't stay in the hotel tonight. Room and board are part of the deal."

I knelt on the floor in front of the bucket. Holding my nose, I leaned forward and dipped my head into the water. It burned like blazes, and I tried to straighten up. But Chief wrapped those long fingers of his around my neck and held me down until I thought my lungs would burst. When he finally loosed his grip, I wheeled around and dunked my head in the tub to rinse off that killer shampoo. If those cooties were still alive, I'd have to cut my head off to get rid of them.

"Well, at least I know what the bad part of the deal was," I gasped.

Chief looked like he wanted to say something, but there was a knock at the door. Jameson stuck his head in and handed Chief a folded uniform. He popped two baseball caps on Chief's head.

"Have him on the porch in five minutes," he said and left.

I was toweling my hair dry as fast as I could. This would be the first time I wore a real uniform, and I didn't want to wait another second. I pulled on my new drawers and a pair of white socks. Chief handed me the jersey. It was gray flannel and would be hot as blazes in the Florida sunshine, but that was no matter. The team name was stitched in red letters across the chest.

"Bloomers?" I asked as I buttoned the jersey. "That's a weird name for a team."

Chief's face looked strange, twisted up like he was bracing himself for an explosion. Then he handed me the rest of the uniform. My mouth dropped open. It was a gray flannel skirt. I stared at Chief. The last item in his hands was a blond wig.

Henrietta Cobb

"**A** girl?" I howled. "I'm supposed to be a girl?"

I dropped the skirt to the floor and leaped for Chief's throat. He grabbed me and wrapped me up in one of those giant arms of his. His other hand held the wig, and he used it to smother my angry yells.

"It's just for one game," he said calmly in my ear. "We get to sleep and eat in the hotel tonight, and we get train tickets to Atlanta. McGraw's there right now."

I went limp in Chief's arms. My anger turned into a weakness that drained me. "I can't do it," I moaned.

"Who's gonna know?" Chief asked. "Nobody here ever saw you before, and they won't recognize you if they see you again."

Chief let me go, and I kicked the skirt across the room. Out from inside it flew a pair of long, frilly bloomers. My heart sank lower.

"It's all about size," Chief said. "If I dressed like a woman, it would put every man in the crowd off marriage for years."

"I can't do it, Chief. Get my clothes back, and let's get out of here. I'll unload wagons until I drop and buy you a train ticket."

"Jameson took your clothes, Hank," Chief answered, looking at the floor. "You leave this room in uniform or in your underwear."

My face burned with anger and shame, but I snatched the bloomers from the floor and pulled them on. I think Chief knew that if he so much as cracked a smile, I'd be at his throat again. "I'll wait outside," he said and set the wig on the floor.

I pulled on the skirt and buttoned it up. It reached my knees, and when I bent down, I could see that a flash of lacy bloomer would show every time I moved. The wig was another torture. That shampoo had left me feeling like I had combed my hair with a blowtorch. The wig ensured that none of the heat could escape.

I clenched my fists and walked to the door, praying that no one would be in the hallway. But that made no sense. In a few minutes I'd be playing ball in front of hundreds of people.

I pulled the door open. Chief kept a straight face. I think he could see the murder in my eyes. He dropped a baseball cap on my head and used pins to fasten it to the wig.

There was a pair of baseball shoes on the floor, and I picked them up and carried them through the lobby. I knew better than to walk across the wooden floor wearing spikes. The clerk ignored us as we passed the desk. I guess he'd seen it all by now.

Jameson was waiting on the porch. I flopped down in a rocker, pulled on the shoes, and tied the laces. It dawned on me that those women and girls I had seen before were my new teammates.

Chief accepted a set of clothes and went back for his turn in the tub. I took a deep breath and started up the street with Jameson. A steady stream of wagons, cars, and trucks stirred up a dust cloud that kept the stares down.

"Hornsby did it, you know," Jameson said.

"Did what?"

"Played for the Bloomers."

My head snapped up. Rogers Hornsby was one of the best young players in the National League. "Are you serious?" I asked.

Jameson nodded. "The secret is to concentrate on who you're playing against, not who you're playing with."

"What would you have done if I hadn't turned up?" I asked.

"I'd have asked one of the town girls to volunteer and stuck her out in right field. But we usually lose when I have to do that."

As we walked through the gate a fan yelled, "Good luck today, darlin'," and my temper flared. Jameson placed a hand on my back and kept me moving forward.

My teammates were already on the field warming up, so I swallowed hard and trotted out to shortstop. Before I could spit, Pinky ripped one at me. I snared it and fired over to first. A little whooshing sound came from the crowd when they saw my throwing arm.

I would never have believed it, but in five minutes I didn't care about the skirt. I was playing on the same field where the big-leaguers had played. I wondered what kind of squad Gainesville would have. Jameson was right. I'd better concentrate on the team I had to play against.

Warmups done, we ran into the dugout. I tried to ignore the hooting and jeering of the fans. The second baseman sat next to me, near enough for our legs to touch. She leaned over to whisper, "Sit with your legs closed. You're wearing a skirt."

I closed them so fast, my knees banged together, and I could feel my face redden.

"Don't be embarrassed," she said, holding her glove in front of her face to hide her words. "My brother is pitching."

She used her glove to point down the bench. From three seats away I could see the Adam's apple bulge from our pitcher's neck. It made me feel better.

Pinky pinned a piece of paper to the wall, and my double play partner went to read the batting order. "Cobb?" she asked when she returned.

I nodded.

"Sally Jameson. You're leading off."

"Mr. Jameson's your dad?"

She nodded.

"I'm Hank," I offered.

"Not today," she said with a smile.

As the visiting team, we'd bat first. I went over to the bat rack. There were four scarred bats, and I pulled out the smallest one. Then I knelt on the top step of the dugout to watch the Gainesville pitcher, a tall right-hander, warm up. All he had was a fastball. Lots of bush leaguers are like that. They throw the ball past a few local boys and figure that's all they'll need. They don't bother to develop another pitch.

The Gainesville players whipped the ball around the infield. Jameson climbed over the railing from his seat by first base and walked onto the field. He held a megaphone in front of his face and announced, "The Traveling Bloomers are honored to play in the up-and-coming community of Gainesville, Florida. I've scoured this great land of ours to assemble my squad. Each young lady is that rare combination of beauty and talent guaranteed to delight and entertain. Let's play ball!"

I took the opportunity to check out the stands. They were already half full, and more people were streaming in. Out in the colored section in right field, families passed picnic baskets back and forth. Most of the white bugs were men, and their mouths were busy with cigars and chaws of tobacco rather than food.

The umpire echoed Jameson's, "Play ball!" and I stepped up to the plate. I was digging in when Jameson's voice boomed through the megaphone, "Batting first for the Traveling Bloomers, shortstop Henrietta Cobb."

Try to concentrate after that! The big farmer on the mound gunned one right down the middle, and I took it for strike one. The crowd's roar woke me up. "Be careful, sweetie! That ball could hurt you," one of the local wits called.

The Gainesville third baseman turned his head toward the stands to acknowledge what a great line that had been. So when the next pitch came in, I pushed a bunt right at him. I ran for all I was worth, my bloomers making little scratchy noises with each stride. My foot slapped against the base a split second before the ball smacked into the first baseman's glove. The umpire hesitated, then bellowed, "Safe!"

A chorus of boos rang out from the stands. Those rubes called the ump every name in the book as he walked out to the pitcher's mound. With me on base, he would stand behind the pitcher to call balls and strikes. The pitcher slammed down the resin bag and muttered something the ump didn't like. The umpire glared until he turned and toed the pitching rubber.

I took my lead toward second. The infielders crept in. Sally was up, and everyone knew she would be bunting to put me in scoring position. The instant the first baseman left the bag, I headed for second.

I took one peek and saw the ball rolling toward first. No way would they come after me. I had too good of a jump. A play Cobb had pulled in Atlanta flashed through my mind, and I sped right on by second base. Pinky was coaching third, and he let loose a stream of curses. But I was committed now.

I dug for third with everything I had, my eyes fixed on the third baseman. He had gotten back to the bag and was waiting for the first baseman's throw. He dipped slightly toward home, so I slid for the outfield side of the bag. He swiped at me, but missed as I skidded past. I wrapped both arms around the base and clung for dear life.

"Safe!" shouted the ump. The bugs erupted in a frenzy.

The wit who had been taunting me switched to yelling at the Gainesville third baseman. "Are you trying to dance with that girl or tag her out?"

The third baseman didn't seem to find the fellow nearly as funny when he was yelling at him. Our pitcher, Sally's brother, was up. "Janet" Jameson, his father called him. He managed to hit a fly ball to center, and I tagged up and scored without having to slide.

"Janet" turned out to be quite a pitcher. Like his dad, he was short and looked as if he hadn't missed a meal in a dog's age. He couldn't throw the ball hard enough to break a window, but he could make it do tricks. One pitch would dart down and away; the next would shoot in on the batter's fists. As the Gainesville batters got more and more frustrated, they swung harder and harder. I almost felt sorry for them.

I did feel sorry for our catcher. She was a solidly built girl who looked like she had done many a hard day's work in the fields, despite Jameson's boast about the beauty of his players. "Janet's" pitches were as hard to handle as they were to hit, and more than once the game was stopped while she shook the pain out of a mangled finger.

I was having so much fun that I forgot about being embarrassed. The Gainesville players hit squibs off the end of the bat and dinks off the handle, so I was busy at short.

In the third inning, a Gainesville batter hit a foul pop behind third. I tore over there, but the ball landed in the bleachers out of my reach. A bug had the ball for about ten seconds. Then a giant hand reached out for it. The bug saw the size of the man that went with it and handed the ball back. The big fellow turned and flipped the ball to me, and I did a double take.

I had forgotten all about Chief. Here he was, in clean clothes, his hair straight and shiny, selling Bloomers' programs in the stands. Baseballs were expensive, and games were often delayed if a bug refused to return a foul ball. Not too many people were going to argue with someone as big as Chief. I guess that's what Jameson had meant about him being useful.

Sally was a marvel at second. She played so smoothly that I kept studying her in the dugout to make sure she was really a girl. But her skin looked too soft, and she smelled too good, even when she was sweating, to be a boy. I wondered what it would be like to play beside her every day. After the games we could sip sodas and talk baseball. Then I remembered I was wearing a skirt. I must look like a complete idiot to her.

Things went smoothly all the way to the eighth inning, the Bloomers clinging to that 1–0 lead. Then the Gainesville batters got smart enough to let a few pitches go by, and the umpire started calling the close ones balls. "Janet" was falling behind the hitters and having trouble with his temper.

A bloop hit and a couple of walks loaded the bases with two down. Mr. Jameson came out and talked to his son while the bugs hooted and yelled for blood. What do you say to your boy when you've got him dressed up like a girl in front of five hundred people? I was desperate and doing it for one day. "Janet" did it all season long. Even my old man had never pulled anything that low.

The stands shook from stomping feet. The bugs yelled insults. The count went full, and "Janet" threw a honey of a curve that came in high but dropped as it crossed the plate. The batter checked his swing, threw down his bat, and started toward first. The umpire began to raise his right arm to call strike three. But the roaring crowd made him reconsider. He signaled ball four, and the score was tied.

"Janet" got so mad that he tore off his cap and threw it on the ground. He had forgotten that his wig was attached. The crowd fell silent for a second, then let out a roar of hatred. Players from the Gainesville dugout came streaming onto the field. The base runners on second and third took advantage of the confusion and raced home. I was frozen in place, until Chief wrapped a huge arm around me and led me back to the dugout.

Sally and the other girls joined us one by one as we watched Pinky and "Janet" duke it out with the angry players. One of the Gainesville players grabbed our big third baseman. But he must have felt something that convinced him she was a genuine girl, because he let her go.

The bugs were screaming their anger, except for the colored folks out in right field. They were chuckling to each other as they packed up their picnic baskets. Since none of their men had been embarrassed and deceived, I guess it was easier for them to see the humor in the situation.

The town constable rode through the gate on the back of a big, black mare. Jameson handed him the megaphone, and he forced his way through the crowd until the horse stood in the middle of the pitcher's mound. "Janet" got up off the ground—muddy and with the beginnings of a shiner. Pinky had kept his feet, but blood was streaming from his nose. Jameson brought him a rag and calmed him down.

The constable put the megaphone to his lips. "Game's over, folks. Final score: Gainesville 3, Bloomers 1. Anybody else starts a ruckus spends the night in jail."

"It's only the eighth inning," I complained.

Chief shrugged and said, "If I were you, I'd concentrate on getting out of here with your wig on."

That sounded like good advice. We stayed on the bench until the crowd thinned. Then Chief walked Sally and me back to the hotel. I asked her if she'd be in the dining room for dinner.

She smiled and said, "I'll be there, but we can't sit together unless you come in uniform. My father's not going to admit that he snuck another ringer onto the team."

My face turned red, and I looked away. First time I felt attracted to a girl, and we were wearing matching outfits. But curiosity got me to ask a question.

"What happened to your regular shortstop?"

"Actually, I'm the shortstop. Our second baseman

ran off with one of the Jacksonville players after our last game. Walked right out of her contract."

"What will you do now?"

"Papa has scouts who'll find someone eventually. He'd sign you up for the season despite those knobby knees," she teased. "We'll be crossing the country."

"No, my skirt-wearing days are over," I said. "Chief and I are trying to catch up with McGraw and the Giants."

By now we were on the porch. When she had pulled off her spikes and straightened up, Sally squeezed my hand. She said, "Good luck, Henrietta," and ran inside before I could react.

Hotel-Guest
Hank

C hief stood there with a smirk on his face while I got out of my spikes. Then he led me through the lobby and up to the second floor of the hotel. Our room was the last one at the end of the hall, looking out on an alley. As soon as the door was closed, I tore off that wig, skirt, and bloomers. There was a pitcher of water, a bowl, and a towel, and I used them to wash off the dirt of the diamond.

Jameson had sprung for new blue jeans, a belt, and a work shirt, all of which were folded on the end of the bed. The jeans were too long, so I rolled up the ends, the cuffs reaching almost to my knees. The denim was so stiff that it dug into my legs when I bent down. But after wearing a skirt, I wasn't about to complain. I buttoned up my new work shirt and stuck my glove inside. Then I realized that I had lost the rock that kept the pocket in my glove.

Chief reached into one of his big pockets and pulled out a baseball. He flipped it to me, and I caught it. It was dinged up, only a rumor of its whiteness remaining, and it had gone spongy on one side from all the hits it had absorbed. But I wouldn't have traded it for anything.

"Thanks, Chief."

"All part of my deal with Jameson," he said. "Let's get to the dinner part."

That dining room was class. Our table was covered with a white cloth, almost clean. A woman brought us a list of foods. I was tempted to order five or six of them, but Chief asked for the roast beef, so I did the same. There were a few flies around, probably the overflow from the diner crowd, but they had better manners. They waited until folks were done eating and settled on the dirty plates.

"What time does the train leave tomorrow?"

"Eight o'clock," Chief answered. "We'll have breakfast here before we go."

Regular meals would be easy to get used to. For a second I thought about staying with the Bloomers. Then I remembered how that wig had tormented me.

After dinner we sat on the porch and rocked. I kept nodding off, so I gave in and went up to our room. The excitement of the last couple of days had caught up with me, and I fell asleep the second I hit the bed.

I was rounding third, tearing for home. The catcher whipped off his mask to take the throw, and I saw that it was my old man. He glared at me with those empty eyes of his, but I couldn't stop. I was sliding right into his grip when fear jerked me awake.

The room was pitch black, and there was no sign of Chief. As my heartbeat slowed, I stopped worrying about the old man and started worrying about Chief. Maybe he had cashed in my train ticket and taken off to find McGraw without me. Or worse, maybe he was using the money to tie on a drunk. I knew that, unlike the old man, some folks were perfectly harmless when they were sober, but turned mean when they drank.

I got out of bed and stumbled across the room. I raised the shade on the window, and a little moonlight crept in. The only weapon I could find was a brass spittoon. I brought it over where I could reach it from the bed, crawled under the covers, and went back to sleep.

Next thing I knew, it was morning. I rolled over, and my face brushed against Chief's big, old, bare foot. That brought me wide awake. I sat up and saw that he had fallen asleep on top of the covers, his head at the foot of the bed. When he felt me stirring, he opened his eyes. There were no signs that he'd been drinking, and I didn't feel comfortable asking him where he'd been.

We splashed our faces with water. Chief shaved with an ancient-looking straight razor he carried in his boot. He nicked himself twice, and by the time he had stanched the blood, we were both starving.

There were newspapers for sale in the lobby, and Chief used three cents of our money to buy us a copy of the Sunday edition of the *Gainesville Daily Sun*. We read the story of the Bloomers game. Jameson apologized for using a male pitcher. He claimed his regular pitcher got sick just before game time and he didn't want to disappoint the fans by forfeiting.

"'The Bloomers' double play combination of Henrietta Cobb and Sally Jameson lived up to their pregame billing,'" Chief read. "'These young ladies were not only attractive, but skilled practitioners of the diamond arts.'"

My face turned red, and I decided I'd heard enough about the Bloomers to last me a lifetime.

"Any news on the Giants?" I asked.

Chief riffled the page. Then his jaw dropped.

"What's the matter?" I asked.

"There was a fire in the Atlanta ballpark, so the Giants' game was canceled. McGraw's headin' north again."

"What'll we do?" I asked.

"Let's take that ride to Atlanta, anyway. At least it's north."

That decided, we went into the dining room for breakfast. I asked Chief for the funny pages. The old man claimed I had taught myself to read by doping out the Sunday comics. I don't know if that's true or not, but I never miss them if I have the chance.

I hadn't seen the Katzenjammer Kids in weeks. They were still playing tricks on the Captain, even though they always ended up getting a whipping in the last panel. If there's a better way to spend a Sunday morning than shoveling eggs down your throat while you read the funnies, I haven't come across it yet.

Chief was buried in the sports, the front page of the paper facing me. I skimmed the headlines. There were stories about the troops coming home now that the Great War was over. The politicians were arguing about how much the German government should pay to make up for the trouble it had caused.

A story in the far right-hand column caught my eye. "Negroes Riot Over Jobs" was the headline. I asked Chief to move his fingers so I could read it. Several hundred Negroes had marched down the street in Washington, D.C., demanding jobs. Seems that during the war, with so many whites off soldiering, Negroes had been hired. Now that the soldiers were returning, the Negroes were losing their jobs. Other Negroes had served in the Army. They felt they had earned the right to be treated as equals, but all the decent jobs were going to whites.

I asked Chief what he thought about the situation.

"If it ain't on the sports page, I don't pay attention to it," was his answer.

We checked out of the hotel, and the clerk handed Chief an envelope with our train tickets in it. I was hoping for a note from Sally, but expected she'd forgotten me already.

It felt strange to walk up to the ticket window at the station. A railroad detective was standing by the tracks, and I nearly bolted when I saw him. Instead of threatening us with his stick, he tipped his hat in greeting. The old man would have swallowed his chaw if he'd been there to see it.

Soon we heard the whistle. The ground started to vibrate before the train came into sight. Then the engine slid past us, steam hissing from her stack and brakes squealing. A cloud of smoke, shoved down by the wind, left us rubbing our eyes.

The train shuddered to a halt, and three passengers got off, their legs wobbling the way legs do when they haven't walked for hours. The conductor came down the steps, and Chief handed him our tickets. He punched a hole in them and gave the stubs back. Chief handed me one, and I stuck it in my pocket as a souvenir. Who knew when I'd be a legitimate passenger again?

Chief let me sit by the window, and I was determined not to miss a thing between here and Atlanta. Most times in boxcars, you have to stay hidden, so there's only so much sightseeing you can do. For once I was free to gawk.

Problem was, miles would roll by with nothing but farms. Towns were an event, so when the whistle blew, I'd straighten up to get a look. But we were rolling at such a pace that we sped by before I could focus my eyes on anything worth seeing.

Chief had brought the newspaper with him. He finally finished memorizing the sports page and gave me a shot at it. Reading about the Giants' prospects in the new season helped the time to pass.

Our one stop was Jacksonville, and we were there just long enough to change trains. Then it was open country again, which combined with the motion of the train to put me to sleep. It was dark when I woke up. Chief dozed until the whistle sounded and the brakes began to squeal.

"Atlanta!" shouted the conductor. "All passengers disembarking in Atlanta should gather their luggage now."

Luggage wasn't something Chief or I had to worry about, so when the train hissed and squealed to a stop, we were the first ones off.

I could tell that Atlanta was a real city, because they had a coffee shop right there at the station. Chief and I spent our last few cents on some biscuits and gravy washed down by coffee so strong, it bent the spoon when you stirred it.

We were trying to figure a way to get farther north when two men slid into the booth behind ours.

"Why do you want to waste your money eating here?" one asked. "I'm saving mine for the carnival."

"If I don't get something to eat, I won't have the strength to get to that carnival," the other replied. "Besides, are you sure they'll be open on Sunday?"

"Positive. Tonight's the last night before they head north."

That was all Chief needed to hear. He raised up and leaned over the back of their booth. I think he scared those fellows a little, though he didn't seem to realize it.

"How do we get to the carnival?" he asked without so much as a howdy.

He was big enough where folks didn't remind him of his manners, so the first man said, "It's on the fairgrounds."

The second one added, "Walk up Peachtree a mile or so and you'll come to it."

Chief headed for the door. I nodded thanks and hustled to catch up. "I didn't know you liked carnivals," I said.

"There'll be a ride north. That's the part I like."

Hank Cobb,
Marksman

S o we walked. It was warm enough to enjoy the evening. After about ten minutes we could see the glow of the lights. Then we heard the calliope squawking, though it was a few minutes more before we could recognize the tune. I had that delicious feeling of not knowing what was coming next. I'd been to my share of carnivals with the old man. He liked to hang out in places where people got careless with their money. Carnivals were seldom dull.

As we got closer the evening came to life with an assortment of dinged-up trucks and cars bouncing down the rutted street. Voices were loud and happy, and Chief and I picked up the pace.

When we reached the fairgrounds, Chief made straight for a guy selling cotton candy.

"Where's the boss?" he asked. "We're lookin' for work."

The candy barker looked him up and down.

"Charlie Conway's his name," he said and pointed across the grounds to a booth where several of the local sharpshooters were trying to win their girls a prize by hitting paper targets. Just as we got there, a man dropped his rifle on the counter, threw his arms up in disgust, and led the group down the Midway.

"You're next, gents," called the man behind the counter. "Step right up and win. Six bull's-eyes gets your choice of prizes."

"We're here to help you skin these rubes, Mr. Conway, not get skinned ourselves," Chief said.

The man grinned and said, "Tell your handle and your scandal."

"Chief Sunrise. I pitch baseballs that no man can hit," Chief answered. "This here's my catcher, Hank Cobb."

This was news to me, though I tried not to show it. I had wanted to see Chief throw the ball, but if he was as good as he said, I wondered if my old mitt could stand up to it.

"Of the Detroit Cobbs, no doubt," Conway teased. "And how do we turn this talent of yours into cash?"

"We charge ten cents a swing," Chief said. "Anyone hits the ball out of the infield wins five bucks."

"My five bucks or yours?" Conway asked.

Chief looked down at this one. "Yours, but it won't happen. I can strike out any man ever held a bat."

"Tell you what, Chief," Conway said. "Tomorrow morning I'll take a look at your stuff. For tonight, take over here. At closing I'll show you where to sleep."

Chief grinned, and we crawled under the counter. Our new boss held a whispered conference with Chief. When he left, Chief started his spiel.

"Step right up and show the marksmanship that drove the buffalo from the plains and left my people weepin'. Win a prize! Six bull's-eyes wins your choice."

"Since when did the Seminoles hunt buffalo?" I asked.

Chief hesitated, then said, "They didn't, but these rubes don't know that."

"What did the Seminoles hunt, anyway?"

"All I know is, this Seminole is huntin' for McGraw. The rest don't matter."

Just my luck. I finally meet an Indian, and he never wants to talk about his tribe.

I looked over the prizes. There were some ratty-looking stuffed animals that might be hard to give away, but there was also a selection of framed pictures of big-league stars. I saw the great Babe Ruth, who had pitched two shutouts in the last World Series, Walter Johnson, Ty Cobb, and a half dozen others. The targets were small, but hitting them didn't look that hard. Still, we worked for an hour, and no one got more than four bull's-eyes.

"Can I try?" I asked during a lull.

"Good idea," Chief said. "But you can't keep the prize."

I was surprised that Chief had such confidence in me. I crawled to the customer side of the counter and picked up one of the .22s. Chief shook his head and handed me

44

a rifle from behind the cigar box that served as a money drawer.

"Use this one, but wait till I get some people here to watch," he said. Chief called out, "Win a prize! The game so easy, even an undernourished boy, runt of the litter, can win."

I felt my face flush, but Chief winked at me. Soon enough his insults attracted a group of locals.

"Show him what you can do, son," they called.

There were ten shots in the rifle, and my first two were misses. Then I found the range and plunked six bull's-eyes in a row. Chief made like he was astonished and reluctantly handed me the picture of Cobb. Ty was sliding into third, spikes flashing, while the third baseman was giving ground.

"Now, run off and show your folks what you won," Chief told me. So I took off down the Midway.

Later, when that crowd had spent its money and gone away empty-handed, I snuck back. "None of them won?" I asked.

" 'Course not," said Chief as he put old Ty back up on the shelf.

I was starting to feel pretty good. Maybe I was a born marksman and didn't know it. I could see myself putting on shows with my trick shooting—in the off-season, of course, when I wasn't playing baseball.

Then Chief said, "Did you figure out how it works?"

I crashed back to earth. The old man would have called me a dummy about now. I looked at Chief as if I had known all along and said, "What's the gimmick?"

"All these rifles have crooked sights. They're bent just enough to throw you off, but not so much that you can notice it. You used the only good rifle, and that stays under the counter."

Our midnight meal consisted of the truck left over from the food stands that lined the Midway. Chief and I chowed down, then curled up under one of the trailers to sleep. By morning my head was itching again, so I figured either I'd picked up another batch of lice or the first batch had survived that horrible shampoo. Remembering how it had felt to stick my head in the bucket, I decided I'd keep the problem to myself.

Breakfast was slim. Everyone ladled oatmeal from a huge pot and guzzled mugs of watery coffee. Then we helped load up the rides and booths so the carnival could move out. I was beginning to think Conway had forgotten all about baseball, when I saw him walking toward us carrying a beat-up catcher's mitt and a bat.

"Get that arm loose," he told Chief. "There's a few in this gang can hit. If you strike them out, we'll give your stunt a try."

He threw me the catcher's mitt. It felt stiff and strange, but I was glad to have it.

We followed Conway across the fairgrounds to a battered diamond. I stayed at home plate. Chief tossed a few soft ones, backing up a step or two after each throw until he had worked his way out to the mound. Then he began to cut loose.

When Chief rared back, all I could see was the sole of his huge, right foot. Then his left arm whipped around and stretched toward me. It seemed that he was halfway to home plate before he let go of the ball.

I'd never seen anything like it. I might have missed the ball completely, it was on me so fast. But it hit my mitt, so I was able to knock it down.

Conway nodded with satisfaction. "Anything besides the fast one?" he asked.

Chief waggled his wrist to show me a curve was coming. When the ball left his hand, it looked high and too far to my right. As I stepped out to catch it, it snapped down and across the plate. I never laid a glove on it.

When I ran the ball down and threw it back to Chief, he called, "Upshoot."

He strode toward first and threw the ball darn near underhand. It started low and rose up as it crossed the plate. I had to leap to catch it, and I could picture a left-handed batter jerking his head back in alarm.

"Let's get a hitter in there," Conway called.

In stepped the cotton candy barker, his sleeves rolled up to show muscular arms. He had a catcher's mask hanging off the end of his bat. I grabbed it and was about to pull it on when Chief waved for me to come out to the mound.

"I'll throw fastballs to this lot," he said when I got there, holding his glove so that the batter couldn't read his lips. "Give me signs to shake off or nod to, but they'll all be smoke."

I turned to go back, and he said, "Hank, keep your bare hand behind you. I don't want you breakin' a finger if someone gets lucky and fouls one."

That was advice I'd remember.

I crouched down and waggled a couple of fingers. Chief shook his head, and I waggled them again. This time he nodded and rared back. The ball slammed into my glove before the candy barker started his swing. Two more, and he was history.

Chief worked his way through every man on that carnival crew. There were a couple of foul tips, one of which smashed into my catcher's mask and left me dizzy. But no one came close to putting the ball in play against him.

When the last batter threw the bat down in disgust, I vaulted out from behind the plate and ran to the mound to shake Chief's hand. He was everything he had bragged of and more.

Conway waited until we had joined him on the third baseline. Then he said, "We'll give it a try."

"What's the terms?" Chief asked.

"Room and board and a free ride north for you and the boy."

"How about a share of the profits?"

"Once we take in the five-dollar prize money, you get a nickel out of every dime."

They shook hands.

We loaded up everything except what little grass was left on the fairgrounds and were on our way by mid-morning. Our little caravan was colorful, with Conway's Carnival painted in bright red letters on the trucks.

I rode in a Ford pickup, which carried a couple of the booths from the Midway. The candy barker, whose name was Pete, drove. Pete was from St. Louis and knew a million stories about the Cardinals and the Browns.

"My father took me to my first game back in aught three," Pete said, smiling at the memory. "The Cards had a rookie pitcher named Mordecai Three Finger Brown. His curve ball had a monstrous break. They were playing the Pirates that day, and he had those boys' knees buckling all afternoon."

"Did he really have three fingers?"

"Yup, on his pitching hand. He said that's what gave him such a hellacious curve ball. He didn't have those extra digits fouling up his grip."

Those miles passed as easily as dandelion fluff sails across the infield on a windy day. Pete explained to me why the Browns had two managers for a while. Branch Rickey managed six days a week, but he had promised his mother he'd never go to the ballpark on Sunday. So whenever the Browns had a Sunday game, their smartest player, Jimmy Austin, would run the team. Next time I started feeling sorry for myself, I'd try to remember that having a mother is not all roses.

Somewhere along the road I dozed off. I dreamed that Chief was running the shooting gallery again, and my old man was a customer. Those crooked sights didn't bother him. Each round tore through the center of a target. The worst part was that each target bore a picture of my face.

Pete was looking at me kind of funny when I jerked awake, so I guess I must have been thrashing around some. But he was good enough to mind his own business. By late afternoon, we were unloading the carnival in a field just outside of Athens.

Working the Crowd

T hings were going great for Chief and me, but my mind kept picking at one thought. How could Chief be this good and not be pitching for somebody? Had he lived so deep in the swamps that no one knew what a great arm he had?

While we were busy setting up the stands and rides, another crew was in town pasting up signs. The carnival would open on the following night and, if we were making money, run for three days. By twilight our share of the work was done. My stomach was screaming that it was suppertime, but Chief insisted that we get the baseball field ready while it was still light out.

He borrowed a can of white paint and a roller that screwed onto a broom handle. I carried a shovel and one of those steel rakes you use for moving dirt around. We walked across the fairgrounds, and Chief painted an arc-shaped line in the grass just past the dirt of the infield.

"If they hit the ball past here on the fly, they win the bet," he explained.

Once the line was drawn, he took the tools from me and started turning over the dirt on the mound.

"You want it soft enough so your foot can get a grip, especially when you don't have spikes."

"Did you pitch wearing those boots back home?"

"They're all I own, so I didn't have much choice," Chief answered.

I was looking for some way to be useful, so I wandered in and inspected the backstop. It had enough holes that if I missed a ball, it was just as likely to go through the screen as to bounce back, but there wasn't anything I could do about that.

Home plate was buried in the dust. I scraped it off with the toe of my shoe, then spat on it a few times to brighten it up. That would give Chief a target to aim at.

"How's your writin'?" Chief asked.

"I haven't used it in a while," I admitted, "but it's good enough to get by."

"First thing in the mornin', I want you to print up a set of rules in nice, big letters. That should cut down on the arguments."

By the time Chief was satisfied with the mound, it was dark. Back at the carnival we grabbed a sausage sandwich from one of the stands. Then I went and found Pete to see if he could remember any more baseball stories.

Next morning Charlie Conway gave Chief a pocketful

of change. We carried it to the bank, where we swapped it for a crisp, five-dollar bill. Then we visited every store in town. Chief issued his challenge, and I displayed the prize money. Since baseball had to be played in the day-light, Charlie Conway would use us to get the townspeople out to the fairgrounds early. That way they'd have plenty of time to spend their money at the carnival.

By lunchtime we were back on the fairgrounds. After murdering a couple of hot dogs apiece, we got to work on the rules. Pete had supplied white paint and an old panel of wood. Across the top I printed a row of dollar signs. Underneath them I wrote:

RISK A DIME—WIN $5!
HIT A FLY BALL PAST THE WHITE LINE TO WIN
ONLY 10 CENTS A SWING

"What other rules are there?" I asked.

"A batter gets one swing and then goes to the end of the line if he wants to try again," Chief said.

This seemed cumbersome to me. "Why not let a man throw us all the dimes he wants and be done with it?" I asked.

"We tell them it speeds up the line," Chief said. "But our real reason is so that no one stays in the box long enough to get their timin' down. Lots of folks can hit a good fastball if they see enough of it."

I painted BATTER MUST GO TO END OF LINE AFTER ONE SWING.

"Anything else, Chief?"

"Yeah, there's no arguin' about whether the ball passed the line or not. That's our call."

I thought of something I had read in the funny papers when they ran a contest to see who could draw the best picture of Krazy Kat. I wrote DESISION OF JUDGES IS FINAL!

Chief looked the board up and down and allowed that I had done pretty well. There was a big, empty space at the bottom, and I offered to draw something there. But Chief took a saw and hacked it off instead.

By four-thirty we were at the field. The contest was set for five o'clock, but some of the town kids were there already, eager to see what Chief had. He warmed up so awkward and slow that it made me nervous. I wondered if something was wrong with his arm.

One boy yelled, "Wish I had a dime. I'd win that five dollars easy."

Chief kept throwing, but he couldn't seem to get loose. By five o'clock half the men in town were lined up, eager for a shot at him, and I was sweating bullets.

I had leaned the rules board against the backstop, and it came in handy to block any pitches that got through me. Conway showed up to collect the dimes, and he read the rules out loud.

"Who's these judges?" somebody yelled out.

"That would be me," Conway answered.

Everyone seemed satisfied, even though Conway was only one person.

That bunch was drooling to get at Chief. He called me out to the mound to pretend to go over the signs, and I couldn't resist asking, "Are you all right?"

"Sure." He smiled. "Why?"

"Your ball's got no pop," I whispered. "McGraw would yank you in a second the way you're throwing."

"That's just to bait the hook, Hank. Better have that glove ready."

I trotted back to home, and the first batter stepped in. He didn't look like much, with a big belly and squinty eyes. Chief threw a medium speed ball up in his face, and he missed it by a foot. While his friends jeered he walked to the end of the line.

I went from being a nervous wreck to pitying those local boys. Chief sized them up perfectly. He threw near the plate, but not over it, to those who looked overanxious. He put on a little extra speed for the batters who drew cheers from the crowd, figuring they were the town's best hitters. He must have earned a hundred dimes before it got dusky dark and people wandered over to the carnival itself. I still hadn't seen a fastball like any he'd thrown the day before.

I carried the mask and the catcher's mitt, and Chief carried the rules. Conway toted the bag of dimes.

"When do we get our share?" Chief asked.

"Soon as we count up the take," Conway said. "But what's going to happen tomorrow? These boys know they can't hit you. Why would they waste good money to try again?"

Chief smiled. "Tomorrow, someone will show up who wasn't here today. These farmers will contact the best player they know so they can see me get my comeuppance."

"Maybe so. But we're not going to make much money off one man."

"We will if we raise the stakes," Chief said.

My eyes got wide. I was nervous enough with five dollars at risk.

Conway grinned. "What did you have in mind?"

"They get a three strike at bat for a buck. Twenty-five dollars to any man hits it out of the infield."

"I hope you know what you're doing," Conway said.

"Keep tonight's money back for good faith," said Chief without even consulting me.

I couldn't tell if we were getting closer to New York or farther away.

Chief's Challenge

I f you want time to pass quickly, a carnival is a good place to be. There's always something that needs putting together or taking apart, loading or unloading. Everything else needs to be repaired. Pete was the carnival's repairman, and he asked me to help him on his rounds. I carried an old leather satchel filled with hammers, saws, screwdrivers, tools I didn't know the names of, and all sizes of screws and nails.

The carnival featured a beat-up carousel that got the kids to nag their parents for a dime. Pete listened to it run for about ten seconds, then yelled to the operator to shut it off. He crawled underneath to work on the engine. My job was easy. I squatted on the grass and slapped tools into his bare hand whenever it snaked out into the daylight.

When Pete finally crawled back out and started the ride up again, it didn't sound much better to me. But Pete seemed happy with the new variety of groans and wheezes it made. He clapped the operator on the back, and we moved on.

It was hotter than blazes that day, but I no sooner mentioned it than Pete recollected a day that was hotter.

"This ain't hot," Pete insisted, sweat streaming down his cheeks. "Why, in Texas last year the hot dogs cooked themselves. All we had to do was brush on mustard and sell them."

There was no end to the stories Pete could tell. Problem was, every time I'd start to enjoy myself, I'd remember that twenty-five-dollar prize. We needed to win that kind of money, not risk giving it out to some-body else. Conway had assigned two men to hang signs all over town, and when they came back to the fair-grounds, they said the challenge was all anyone could talk about.

And that was only one problem. Every day we were delayed in getting to New York was another day McGraw had to set his team for the season. I checked with Pete, and he said it was April 9. Opening day was the fourteenth.

Chief and I got over to the diamond at four-thirty, and half the town was there waiting. Everybody was talking and laughing. Seeing them so cheerful and confident made me feel like choking up the cotton candy Pete had given me for lunch.

Chief didn't seem to notice, though. He went through his same warm-up routine. By the time Charlie

Conway started going over the rules, we were surrounded by people. Folks sat along both baselines, close enough to get creamed by a foul ball. The wire of the backstop was humming from all the fingers stuck through the mesh, moving it back and forth.

There wouldn't be any need for Charlie Conway to rule whether a fly ball was long enough to win the prize. Spectators ringed the infield, their toes touching the white line of paint. Any ball hit into the crowd would win the money.

The mayor of Athens stood right behind Chief, watching him warm up. Every couple of minutes, someone would push through the crowd and hand the mayor a dollar. He would write the person's name in a little notebook he carried. The pile of money was growing, but no one lined up to hit, and we didn't see anyone swinging a bat.

Chief met me halfway between home plate and the pitcher's mound, where we could talk without being overheard.

"They've got somethin' cooked up," he said, not looking the least bit worried. "If I touch my cap, I'm throwin' a curve. If I spit on the ground, the upshoot is comin'. You give fake signs like yesterday."

The sticky weather had Chief's hair curling up again like it had when we were loading that train in Gainesville. He didn't look nearly as mean as he did when it was straight.

The folks in the outfield started to shout. The noise spread through the crowd, building into a wall of sound.

Bodies drew apart to let a man pass through. First all I saw was a battered ball cap. Then I made out a craggy face—an Indian like Chief. As he came nearer I saw that he was limping. Instead of a cane, he leaned on a massive baseball bat, which shone from the loving attention it had enjoyed. My heart sank when I recognized him.

"That's Joe Lightfoot!" I managed to croak. "He's a major-leaguer." I could picture the Zee-Nut Candy Bar card I had once had that showed Joe pointing the barrel of his bat at the camera like a rifle.

"We're headin' for the majors, Hank," Chief said calmly. "I can get him out."

The roar from the crowd grew as Joe Lightfoot made his way toward home plate. Joe was a great athlete, having won two gold medals running footraces in the Olympics. When the Olympic Committee found out he had been paid money for playing baseball, they took the medals back. My old man said it was typical. A bunch of rich folks make a rule that a poor man can't cash in on the one thing he's good at.

Joe Lightfoot never said much about it. He returned the medals and started playing in the big leagues. He had been a star for the past five years, and I couldn't figure out what he was doing here.

"Why is he limping like that?" I asked Chief.

"He broke his leg slidin' into home last September. Looks like it hasn't healed right. He can't play in the big leagues if he can't run."

But he wouldn't have to run to win our twenty-five dollars, I thought.

Lightfoot reached home plate. He turned in a circle, waving to his fans. Then he took a few practice swings, which earned another roar. The mayor handed Charlie Conway one of the dollar bills, called out the name of the first bettor, and we were ready to start.

Lightfoot stepped into the batter's box, sighted down the bat at Chief, and took his stance. I squatted behind the plate, giving my meaningless signs. Chief fired a fastball, twice the speed of any he had thrown yesterday. It was a little outside, and Lightfoot let it go by. Chief brought another speed ball, and Lightfoot's bat whistled past my mask. It was a hard grounder between short and third—maybe a base hit in a game—but an out by our rules. I didn't know whether to be relieved that we had one out, or nervous that Joe Lightfoot had gotten around on the fastball so easily.

The mayor dropped another dollar into Conway's hand, announced another name, and we started over. This time, Chief adjusted his cap before starting his windup, so I knew the curve was coming. Lightfoot tried to check his swing, but he couldn't stop. The ball dove straight for the ground, and he missed it badly.

He leaned over the plate, so Chief spat and threw the upshoot. Lightfoot started his swing, and the ball kept bearing in on him. His rear end was headed toward Florida as the bat moved toward New York. The ball bounced off the handle for an easy out.

The mayor dropped another dollar. Lightfoot muttered something to himself and stepped out long enough to take a couple of measured practice swings. He should have stayed out of the box, because Chief threw a lively fastball that Lightfoot popped straight up in the air.

Chief stepped off the mound and raised his glove. Then, at the last second, he whipped his cap off his head and caught the ball in that. Some of the bugs cheered him, but Lightfoot seemed annoyed by the showmanship. He banged his bat on the ground and dug in again.

The mayor kept feeding Conway dollars, and Chief kept firing pitches to Joe Lightfoot. Watching how coolly Chief handled himself had me believing he might really be good enough to pitch for McGraw.

The crowd got quieter as each dollar changed hands. Then, the way people will, a few of them started cheering for Chief. The noise was getting quite respectable, when Lightfoot hit a little foul pop that I caught along the first baseline.

All eyes turned to the mayor, but he shook his head and showed the crowd his empty palms. Nine dollars had changed hands, and Lightfoot hadn't come close to winning the prize.

The crowd was stirring, gathering itself to head for the carnival or home, when Joe Lightfoot stuck two fingers in his mouth and cut loose with a shrill whistle that set the wax to tingling in my ears.

Everyone froze. Very deliberately, Joe Lightfoot squatted down and unlaced his right shoe. He pulled it off, reached inside, and brought out a folded bill. He opened it up, and I gasped to see that it was five dollars.

"How about it, Chief?" Lightfoot called. "One more chance. My five-dollar bill against your hundred."

My blood ran cold. You could have bought Charlie Conway's whole outfit for not much more than a hundred bucks.

Chief nodded his head.

The crowd roared as I took the bill from Joe Lightfoot's hand and ran it out to the mayor. Folks were back on Joe's side now that he was risking his own money instead of theirs. Joe Lightfoot, shoe tightly relaced, spat in his palms. He gripped the bat, then waggled the head at Chief as if signaling him that the game was on.

Chief wound and threw a blinding fastball. Joe Lightfoot swung, and the crack of the bat caused my heart to sink in my chest. But I heard a second slap an instant later and looked up to see Chief squeezing the ball in his mitt. Lightfoot's line drive would have soared into the outfield if it had gotten by, but Chief had speared it.

The crowd went wild. Folks stormed the mound and pounded Chief on the back as if they had been rooting for him the whole time.

My knees were wobbling. I felt almost sick with happiness. All I wanted to do was get our money and leave. The old man always told me to quit when I was ahead, and as much as I hated to admit it, his advice seemed awfully sound.

Conway was so happy with the fourteen dollars Chief had won that he kept punching him in the shoulder. He didn't even seem to mind that thunder had begun to rumble and most of the crowd was headed for home instead of for the carnival.

Joe Lightfoot hobbled out to the mound and shook hands with Chief.

"Great stuff and a good glove besides. That's the best pitching I've seen since I left the majors," he said. "You and your catcher come have dinner with me, and we'll talk about getting you a tryout. I still have friends in the bigs."

Chief smiled and mumbled thanks. I had all I could do to stand still. Maybe it was because he was an Indian, but Chief didn't show much excitement.

"What tribe are you from?" Lightfoot asked. "Someone said Seminole, but I never saw a Seminole wear his hair like you do."

Chief looked as if he didn't feel too well. "Hank and I will go get cleaned up. Where should we meet you?" he asked.

"I'll be in the Peachpit Café, down the street. Do you favor ribs?"

My mouth started watering at the thought. Much as I liked hot dogs and sweets, carnival food was starting to wear on me a little. Chief nodded and shook Joe's hand again.

The first drops of rain fell as we walked back toward the carnival with Conway.

"Let me have our money for last night and today," Chief said. "Hank and I are takin' off."

I guessed that Chief figured Joe Lightfoot was our big chance.

Conway stopped. "But, Chief, this is only the beginning. We can run this game in every town. You'll have a ton of money by the time you get to New York."

"That's just it. When does the carnival hit New York?"

"I'll have to check, but sometime early in June," Conway answered.

"We can't wait," Chief said. "I want to get to McGraw now, before the season starts. We're leavin' tonight."

Conway sighed and counted out our money. He paid what he owed us from the first night, plus seven dollars from the battle with Joe Lightfoot. He started to pocket the rest of the money, thought better of it, and handed me a dollar.

"Thanks, Mr. Conway," I said.

"You kept Joe Lightfoot off balance the way you mixed up those pitches. I was watching your signs, and I couldn't figure out what was coming."

"He's a good catcher, all right," Chief said with a straight face.

"If things don't work out with Joe Lightfoot, you're welcome to come back," Conway said.

We all three shook hands and picked up our pace as the rain began to pelt down. Chief's hair was curlier than ever after walking through the rain. My scalp was itching, so I planned to leave my cap off and try to drown those cooties on the way back into town.

Conway let us use his trailer to clean up. Chief stood in front of the mirror that hung over Charlie's wash basin.

"Time we both took care of our hair," he said. "I seen you scratchin'."

"Stay away from me with that shampoo," I warned. "That stuff almost killed me last time."

But Chief wasn't reaching for shampoo. He picked up a pair of scissors and chopped at his hair. It fell to the floor in curly bunches. Then he pulled his straight razor from his boot and began shaving the sides of his head.

I watched, my mouth hanging open. In minutes Chief had no hair left except for a thin patch running down the middle of his scalp.

"Do I look like a Seminole now?" he asked.

I nodded, though I wasn't sure what a Seminole looked like.

"Your turn," Chief said. "Come on over here."

Anything sounded better than that shampoo. But I held back. "Can't it wait until after we eat at the café?" I asked.

Chief sighed. "We're not goin' to the café. Soon's we're ready we're headin' north."

If one of those head lice had bitten at that moment, it would have knocked me over.

"What do you mean, Chief? Joe's going to set us up," I pleaded. "Not to mention the ribs."

"We don't need Joe Lightfoot or anybody else. I've got the arm, and that's all that matters."

I tried to think of more arguments, but it's hard to reason with someone who's running a razor over your scalp. In about ten minutes, I was bald as an egg. At least my head didn't itch anymore.

We grabbed a last hot dog on our way off the grounds

and headed for the train station. The rain was warm, which was good, since with no hair to stop it, it dripped off my ball cap and down the back of my neck.

A kid about my age hawked up a phlegm ball and sent that sailing out the window of a pickup truck at us. But it went wide. It's hard to time something like that when you're clipping along at a good rate. Everyone else ignored us. When we reached the station, Chief bought two tickets on the first train heading north.

A Beeline for New York

Those few dollars got us as far as Raleigh, North Carolina. There we spent most of our remaining money on bacon and eggs, before sneaking into a boxcar to continue our trip north.

In two days we were broke, but we were in Wilmington, Delaware, only a couple of hundred miles from New York. We had nearly caught up to McGraw. The Giants were in Philadelphia that drizzly afternoon, playing an exhibition game against Connie Mack's Athletics. If we could catch one good ride, we'd arrive in New York tomorrow, the same day as McGraw, and the day before the season opener.

We skulked around the rail yards all day, twice getting rousted by railroad detectives. Each time a northbound freight stopped, we tried to sneak on, but either we were spotted and had to run for it, or the boxcars were locked up tight.

By late afternoon Chief had lost his patience. "Let's walk out to the road and hitch a ride to another town. Maybe we can find a rail yard that's not watched so close."

I was tired and didn't feel like standing on the side of the road, so I said, "Let's make one more pass through the yard. If we don't find anything, we'll try your idea."

Chief eyeballed me. "All right, but we're goin' to find out why railroad cops carry sticks if they catch us."

Chief and I crept through the freight yard, careful to stay behind shipping containers and maintenance sheds whenever we could. We had worked our way nearly to the end of a long freight when we heard a commotion.

Two men were trying to convince a horse to walk up a wooden ramp and into a boxcar. The horse wanted no part of it. Her eyes were wild, foam flew from her lips, and she reared against the ropes with which they tugged her.

We stopped, more to watch the show than with any hope of a ride. The horse twisted her head violently, pulling the rope out of one man's hands. In a split second, she had charged at the other man, causing him to drop his rope and run in fear. Both men followed as the horse galloped through the rail yard. Chief and I were alone.

"C'mon," Chief said.

He sprinted across the yard, up the ramp, and into the boxcar with me close behind. When my feet left the ramp and hit the boxcar floor, they sank into a knee-deep layer of hay. I was so surprised that I lost my balance and pitched forward into the backs of Chief's legs.

Chief barely noticed. As I picked myself up his eyes were scanning the car. He stumbled through the hay and pulled up the lid on a wooden crate. It was filled with apples. He stuffed some in his shirt and motioned for me to do the same.

By the time my shirt bulged with apples, Chief had made his way to the rear of the car, where the hay was mounded nearly to the ceiling. He began to burrow into the haystack.

"You can't be serious," I said. "What if they load that wild horse in here? She's liable to kick us through the wall."

"I'd rather face a horse than a railroad detective," Chief answered. "We've got food," he added, waving an apple, "and a soft place to lie down. What more can two bums ask?"

So I burrowed in, too. We dug our way to the back of the car. Chief pulled out his razor and started carving a small hole in the wall with the blade.

"Ventilation," he said.

I'd have to remember to cover my eyes next time he tried to shave with that thing.

We heard voices. The car rocked as hoofs beat on the wooden ramp. The horse made a soft, whickering noise as if there were nowhere she would rather be than on a freight train.

"That's my girl. Cappy will take care of his Beeline," came a soft murmur.

"I don't know how you do it," another voice said. "Buck and I couldn't load that horse for nothing, yet she walks right into the car for a half pint like you."

"Why would you try to load Beeline without her jockey? A man stops for a sip of whiskey to wash the dryness from his throat, and no one has the patience to wait for him," Cappy complained.

"That throat of yours hasn't had a chance to get dry in the five years I've known you," said a different voice that I figured was Buck's. "Besides, if you'd have been much later, the train would have left without you."

"I made it, and I've got my bottle to shorten the ride," said Cappy. "Now get out of here so Beeline and I can get settled."

The screech of the door sliding along its track caused Beeline to whinny nervously, but Cappy's soothing voice soon had her calm again.

"Let's hope they've learned their lesson this time, eh, girl? Beeline won't listen to anyone but Cappy, will you?"

The dust from the hay was tickling my nose, and I pinched my nostrils between two fingers. No way was I going to make it to New York without sneezing.

A gurgling sound was followed by a satisfied, "Ahh! That hit the spot, Beeline." A bottle dropped to the floor with a clank. There was silence except for the sound of Beeline's hoofs shuffling through the hay. Then I heard Cappy snoring.

A nap seemed like a good idea, and I was settling into a doze when the hay stirred. At first I thought Chief was restless, but a crunching, grinding sound made me realize Beeline was eating her way toward us. I wasn't worried. By the time she ate all the hay between us and her, we'd be in New York.

But then Beeline snorted and started plowing through the haystack. I froze, but she kept coming until, suddenly, her massive teeth sank into the front of my shirt. That brought me up out of the hay with a shout. I didn't mind apple juice running down my belly, but I needed this shirt, and besides, the next bite might damage my mitt.

It's not a good idea to startle a horse, especially in an enclosed space like a boxcar. Beeline reared and whinnied. Cappy jumped up, tripped over his pint whiskey bottle, and fell headfirst into the hay.

I pressed up against the back wall of the boxcar in terror. Cappy regained his feet and tried to soothe Beeline. A hand bumped against my leg from inside the haystack, scaring me again. But it was Chief, holding out an apple.

I lay the apple flat on my palm and took a nervous step forward. Beeline's nostrils flared, but her eyes lost their wild look. She pawed the floor a time or two with her hoofs, then pursed her lips and plucked that apple from my hand as gentle as you please. She chomped. Juice oozed from the sides of her mouth, and she stepped forward for more.

Quick as I could, I opened my shirt and lay the mashed and whole apples in the hay. Then, as she ate, I stepped gingerly around her only to find myself face to face with Cappy.

Cappy was no taller than me, but he had a mean look in his eye that had taken a lot more than my fifteen years of life to develop. I had expected him to be startled, but I didn't understand the hatred in his glare until he spoke.

"So, they've snuck another jockey in behind Cappy's back. It'll take more than apples to make Beeline run for you. Fight like a man. If you whip me, Beeline is yours."

He put up his puny fists and began dancing around as if in a boxing ring. "Come on. Fight for your mount, boy."

"I'm no jockey," I protested, pulling out my mitt. "I'm a ballplayer, hitching a ride to the Polo Grounds in New York."

Cappy sneered and spat on the floor. "Are they the New York Midgets now? I know your sport, and it's not baseball. Come take your whipping."

I didn't move, so Cappy charged at me, uncorking a wild right. I jumped aside, and he sailed into the haystack, where he got tangled up with Chief. Before I knew it, Chief stood, brushing hay off himself with one hand, an infuriated Cappy dangling from the other.

"Now you're a giant!" Cappy howled, looking up at Chief. "They've snuck in a jockey and a giant."

"I'm not a Giant yet," Chief announced, setting Cappy down in the hay, "and Hank's no jockey. We're hitchin' a ride to New York to meet Mr. John McGraw. That's the only reason we're in this car."

"I know a jockey when I see one," Cappy insisted.

I sighed. Would I ever grow to a respectable size?

Chief said, "Hank, step forward here, and hold out your hands."

I did as I was told. Beeline had finished the apples and was munching the juicy patch of hay they had lain on.

"See the paws on that boy?" Chief asked Cappy. "Boys are like pups. Those big hands tell you he's gonna grow. He's no jockey, just a runty ballplayer."

Cappy seemed unconvinced, so I pulled one foot up out of the hay.

"Is it a man's shoe you're wearing, boy?" Cappy asked. "For sure no jockey ever had feet like that. The pair of them would put you over the weight limit."

Chief stuck out his hand and introduced himself.

"Chief Sunrise, greatest Indian to ever pitch a baseball."

"Casper O'Connell," responded Cappy, his hand disappearing in Chief's grip, "champion jockey and master horseman. People call me Cappy."

"Hank Cobb, future major-leaguer," was my line.

Cappy looked suspiciously at the haystack. "If I poke a pitchfork in there, will the rest of the team come out?"

"There's just me and Hank," Chief assured him. "Does this train pass through Manhattan?"

"It does indeed. Beeline is on her way to Belmont Park. You're welcome to ride along if you pay your fare. Otherwise, I'll have you put off at the next station."

Chief looked down.

"Me and Hank are broke," he admitted. "That's why we snuck in the car."

Cappy considered this. "Usually ballplayers don't go broke until after the races. You boys are the first I've known to tap out before the horse even gets to the track."

"Maybe we could earn our ride," I offered. "It must be a lot of work to care for a big animal like Beeline."

Cappy grinned. "Now you're talking, lads. By the time we get to New York, you'll have learned how to tend a horse from the master."

That didn't sound bad, so the three of us shook hands again.

Cappy's idea of training was to sit on a wooden crate, reading the sports page and sipping rotgut, while Chief and I cleaned up after Beeline. I had no idea a horse could produce that much manure in a five-hour train ride. Maybe it was the apples.

At last the train stopped at the Hudson River Station in New York, and Cappy gave us directions for walking to the Polo Grounds. Chief cracked open the door, peeked outside, and nodded to signal that no one was in sight.

"Good luck, men," Cappy called as we walked off, "and if McGraw does take you on, bring your paycheck to the track and bet on Cappy and Beeline."

Cleaning a Cement
Bathtub

We had finally made it. After sleeping in a park overnight, Chief and I stood in the morning sunlight staring down at the Polo Grounds from the top of the hill the locals called Coogan's Bluff. I don't know who Coogan was, or what he might have been bluffing about, but spread out below us was the real thing.

The Polo Grounds reminded me of a cement bathtub with none of the sagging grace of the old, wooden ballparks I was used to. But the size was impressive. You could have set Gainesville Park, stands and all, in center field.

"Why do you suppose they made it out of cement?" I asked Chief.

"The wooden park burned down," he explained. "This one's here to stay."

The grass was lush, the infield was raked to perfection, and my mind reeled with the thought that big-leaguers played here.

Then the Giants came popping out of the dugout. While we gawked, players loosened up their arms, played pepper, stretched their muscles in the spring sunshine. Another group, probably the pitchers, began running laps along the outfield fence. The fences were covered with colorful signs, though we were too far away to read their messages.

A short, round man stood near the pitcher's mound, arms folded, taking it all in. He gestured at one group, then another, waving impatiently. It had to be McGraw.

"Do you see him?" I asked Chief.

"Let's get down there," was his response.

We followed a winding stairway down the bluff to the huge stadium and stopped where a line of boys waited at one of the side entrances.

"What's goin' on?" Chief asked.

The last boy on line, who looked even grubbier than we did, whipped around, a snarl on his lips. When he saw Chief, he remembered his manners.

"Season starts tomorrow. They're hiring boys to clean the seats," he said.

I got on line. Chief and I were broke, the work sounded easy, and I would have a better chance to meet McGraw inside the stadium than out here on the street.

Chief said, "I'm goin' to ask around the neighborhood, see what I can find out about McGraw's routine. We'll meet back here later."

He crossed the street with that gangling gait of his and struck up a conversation with a man who was piling potatoes onto a wooden display outside a market.

I stood for ten minutes or so staring at the other boys and the concrete wall. Then a man wearing black pants and a white shirt unlocked the gate. A straw boater was cocked crookedly on his head, as if he were so busy, he couldn't even take the time to straighten his hat. He led us inside and lined us up on a cement walkway. Then he paced up and down, looking us over.

We couldn't see the diamond, but the repeated crack of bat on ball told me that the Giants were taking batting practice. I was itching to run and not stop until I reached the field. But that would get me thrown out and ruin our chances.

"My name's O'Hara," the man announced. "I'm looking for a few boys who know how to work and work hard."

As he talked he walked down the line. He tapped about half the boys on the shoulder and pointed his thumb at the gate. They mumbled insults and went back outside.

When he got to me, the last in line, he hesitated. His hand stretched out, and I said, "Don't go by size, sir. I can outwork anyone here."

O'Hara pulled back his hand and smiled. "We'll find out, son," he muttered, then turned to the group. "If any of you are here to watch the ballplayers, save us both some time and leave now. You'll be too busy."

This didn't scare anyone away. I'm sure the rest of the boys, like me, figured they'd find a way to work and watch at the same time.

O'Hara had us wait while he relocked the gate. Then he led us down a dark corridor, the cement throwing off a dampness that made me glad to keep moving. We came to a pile of empty potato sacks, and O'Hara gave us two apiece. We walked up a ramp and got our first view of the field.

Up close, and after the darkness of the stadium's innards, the grass looked too green to be real. We gaped at the players running down fly balls, backhanding grounders, and slinging baseballs across the diamond. O'Hara didn't let us look long. He marched us around the stadium, stopping to assign each boy a section of seats to clean.

"Wipe down every chair, back and seat, top and bottom. I'll be spot-checking later, and if I find any rows you've skipped, you'll be out on the street," he warned.

Since I was the last boy hired, I followed O'Hara all the way out to the center field bleachers for my assignment. The sign on the outfield wall said we were 473 feet from home plate. A few players were jogging on the grass, and this far from the batter, it wasn't likely anyone would hit a ball that would threaten them.

I climbed all the way to the top row and started rubbing down the wooden benches. I tried to work facing the field, watching the players, but I was so high up that it made me dizzy. I turned around and worked facing the bench I was wiping.

It was easy work. The wood was freshly painted, and all I had to do was dust it off. You think of a ballpark as a noisy place, but today it was peaceful. The crack of bat on ball, the slap of ball on leather, the chatter of the coaches and players—all seemed muffled in the huge stadium.

When my back started aching, I sat and looked at what I had accomplished. Four rows were dusted, and I had dozens to go. I started wondering how long this would take and how much the pay would be.

The Giants knocked off for the day long before I reached the bottom row along the outfield fence. O'Hara was sitting there waiting for me. He gave me a ham sandwich, which went down in two bites. Then he walked me back through the stadium.

"You're the last one done, kid, but you had the most work to do. I like the way you stuck with it," he said.

He handed me a dollar wrapped around a small piece of cardboard. It was a ticket for a bleacher seat for the next day's game.

"At least you know the seat will be clean," he joked.

"Mr. O'Hara," I asked, "do you have any jobs for during the season?"

"They're for men," he said. "I use boys for the part-time stuff. Aren't you in school?"

"I'm older than I look," I said, hoping that would satisfy him. "Anyway, I was asking for my guardian."

O'Hara reached into his shirt pocket and pulled out another ticket. "Bring him to the game tomorrow. I'll meet you at noon right where you came in today."

We shook hands, and I ran back out of the stadium to look for Chief. I found him a block away, sweeping the sidewalk in front of a saloon.

"McGraw lives in the hotel up the street," Chief reported. "As soon as I finish, we'll wait around there until he comes home. Then we'll talk to him."

"Where are we sleeping tonight?" I asked.

"I'm earnin' us a room right now," Chief said, "over the saloon."

By the time Chief was done sweeping, I'd updated him on my news.

"You got the money for our supper, and I got us a place to sleep," Chief said. "Now let's go meet McGraw."

The Gotham Hotel was a five-minute walk from the Polo Grounds. McGraw and many of the Giants' players lived there all season long. On game days, every kid in the neighborhood would be out to yell his greetings as the players made their way to the ballpark. Chief had learned all this and more talking to the workers in the businesses that lined the block.

We walked up and down the street, first on one side, then the other, always staying in sight of the hotel's main entrance.

"If we sit on the steps or just stand around, the doorman will run us off," Chief explained.

My stomach was growling, and I kept rubbing my fingers against the dollar in my pocket to remind myself that food was coming. At least I'd had a sandwich in the stadium. For all I knew, Chief hadn't had any food since Beeline's apples, and he was a lot bigger than I was.

At last we saw a short man in an expensive suit and bowler hat making his way up the sidewalk. Chief straightened his ball cap, tucked in his shirt, and crossed the street to intercept him.

"Mr. McGraw?" he called out.

McGraw waved a greeting and picked up his pace.

"Mr. McGraw," Chief repeated, "can I talk to you a minute?"

McGraw stopped and turned to face Chief. I was trailing a few steps behind, not knowing whether my presence would help or hurt the situation.

"I've had a busy day," McGraw said, his eyes running up and down Chief's long body.

"This'll only take a minute," Chief promised. "Name's Chief Sunrise, best pitcher you ever saw, the greatest Indian ever to set foot on a diamond. I want to play for the Giants."

McGraw looked at Chief's dirty clothes and laughed. "It doesn't look like you've been too successful so far, Chief. The Giants have open tryouts at the end of June. Watch the newspapers for the date."

He started to walk away, but Chief stepped in front of him. McGraw glared.

"We're done talking. Move aside," he demanded.

"But, Mr. McGraw," Chief insisted, "I'm the real thing. Let me throw for you, and you'll see I'm not lying."

A uniformed man strode past me, stick gripped in his right hand. The old man would have skinned me good if I had let a cop sneak up on him that way.

"Is there a problem, Mr. McGraw?" he asked, tapping the stick in his left palm.

"Good evening, Hennesy," McGraw said. "I believe this gentleman was just leaving."

Chief started to speak, thought better of it, and stuffed his hands in his pockets. He made a wide circle around Officer Hennesy and walked back toward our room.

Opening Day

We were waiting for O'Hara at the side gate of the Polo Grounds at noon the next day. Chief was feeling down, trying to think of what he could have said to make McGraw give him a chance. But being in a big-league stadium on opening day had me excited.

We'd both cleaned up the best we could. Chief had wanted to shave my head again, but I wouldn't let him near me with that chewed-up razor of his. He had his Seminole strip back, but with all the nicks he'd given himself, it looked like someone had tried to scalp him.

I introduced Chief to O'Hara, and I could tell right away that O'Hara was impressed with his size.

"I've got the perfect job for you," O'Hara said. "There's a group that call themselves the Sportsman's Club, but what they really are is a bunch of drunks and gamblers. They sit along the third baseline. Whenever one of them gets a foul ball, they refuse to give it back. Do you think you're up to dealing with them?"

"By the end of the game, they'll be throwin' the ball back before I even get to them," Chief promised.

O'Hara took Chief to get a cap and shirt that would show that he worked for the Giants. We agreed to meet at the gate after the game. I was free to watch some baseball.

With an hour until game time, the crowd was trickling in. The visiting Cincinnati Reds were taking batting practice. Baseballs were whizzing around the field so fast, I didn't know where to look first.

On my way out to the bleachers, I stopped to read the signs I had noticed from up on Coogan's Bluff. The Giants' left fielder was named George Burns, and the sign painted on the left field wall made me laugh out loud. It read, "Last year George Burns caught 198 flies, but Ajax Flypaper caught 19 billion, 865 million."

If I had extra cash, I'd buy a package of Ajax Flypaper and send it to that diner down in Gainesville. They'd set a new record fast in that place.

I settled into the first row of the bleachers. It was cloudy, and the breeze had a bite to it, but there was nowhere on earth I would rather have been. At long last, I was going to see my first big-league game.

The Giants came out for their turn at warming up. Art Fletcher was the shortstop, and I remembered that he was one of my old man's favorite players. Suddenly I felt guilty. Suppose the old man had been hurt falling from the train? What if those men chasing after us had shot him? What kind of a kid would let his own father fall when he could have helped him?

But then I thought of all the things my father had done to me: the beatings for no reason, the times he'd made me steal and cheat. I hadn't broken a law, other than sneaking rides on trains, since I got away from him. Didn't I have the right to lead an honest life?

I unbuttoned my shirt and pulled out my ball and glove. If I'd done wrong, why did I have nightmares about the old man coming back? I pounded the ball into my glove harder and harder until my aching palm drove all thoughts of anything outside this ballpark from my mind.

It was nearly game time, both teams in their dugouts, when the boom of a bass drum announced the arrival of the Sportsman's Club. They must have been a hundred strong as they marched in, led by the drummer. They paraded through the stands to the last empty section in the huge ballpark. When they reached their reserved seats behind third base, the drummer stepped aside. The Sportsmen filed past him to fill the rows, but remained standing, marching in place until each club member was in front of his seat. Then with a final boom from the drum, they let out a cheer for the Giants and settled into their seats.

My eyes scanned the area, looking for Chief, but even a big fellow like him would be hard to spot in this crowd. There were more people in the stands than lived in most of the towns and cities I'd spent time in. A roar from the crowd snapped my head around, and I watched the Giants run onto the field. They went about their business as smoothly and professionally as if they weren't being observed by thousands of screaming bugs. When you've won as many pennants as they had, it takes a lot to rattle you.

The Giants' starting pitcher was a right-hander named Jesse Barnes. Last year he had been a soldier fighting in Germany. Now McGraw was calling him the ace of the staff. I was a long way from home plate, but it seemed to me that his stuff couldn't compare with Chief's. If only there was some way to get McGraw to watch Chief throw.

Barnes and the Reds' pitcher, Ray Fisher, had the upper hand on the batters. Each team managed a few base runners, but the game was scoreless after four innings. Leading off the fifth, the Reds' Edd Roush slapped a foul ball into the seats behind third. The Sportsman's Club stood and cheered as one of their members leaped high in the air and snagged the ball. He had barely landed when the members wrapped their arms around each other as if in an enormous huddle. When they threw their arms in the air and let loose another cheer, the ball had disappeared.

How did O'Hara expect Chief or anyone else to get a ball back from that bunch? How could he figure out who had it? I turned my attention to the field. Roush took the next couple of pitches for balls. Then the fans let out a roar that had nothing to do with the ball game. Roush stepped out of the batter's box and peered up into the stands.

My eyes went back to the Sportsman's Club. A tall man in a Giants cap—it had to be Chief—was holding one of the club members upside down and shaking him. The other members were howling, but so far none had come to the rescue of their fellow Sportsman.

As I watched, Chief dropped the guy none too gently to the floor and grabbed the Sportsman sitting behind him. In a second, he was hanging upside down, gripped by the ankles with Chief's huge hands. Lots of stuff fell from his pockets, but apparently no baseball, because Chief tossed him aside, too.

Then a fellow two rows back bolted from his seat. He ran up the steep stairs of the stadium with Chief in hot pursuit. The crowd roared with excitement at the chase. The Sportsman might have been a drinker as O'Hara said, because before he reached the top of the stairs, he was slowing down. Despite his head start, he couldn't outdistance Chief. Chief dove and brought him down with a solid tackle.

They scuffled briefly. Chief stood and waved the recovered baseball over his head. Then came the amazing part. Time was out on the field as the players and umpire were watching the action in the stands. Chief yelled, "Hey, Barnes!" and whipped the ball over the heads of the bugs. It soared past the dozens of rows of seats, past the dugout, and all the way to the pitcher's mound, where it smacked into a startled Jesse Barnes's glove with a slap that rang through the ballpark.

At first the fans were as stunned as Barnes. But when Barnes pulled off his mitt to shake the pain from his hand, they let out a roar that shook the stadium and made me glad it was built of cement. Chief tipped his cap and melted into the crowd so the game could resume.

Exciting as the game was, nothing the players on the field did could match Chief's throw. The Reds won 1–0, the only run scoring on an error by first baseman Hal Chase.

I met Chief where we had come into the stadium. The bugs streaming past yelled comments about his arm. We waited for O'Hara until the place was almost empty. Then he came down the corridor on the run.

"McGraw wants to see you," he shouted. "He can't believe the way you threw that ball!"

"I tried to tell him yesterday, but he wasn't in the mood to listen," Chief said with his usual deadpan expression.

O'Hara led us down to the field. We hopped over the low railing near third base and stepped into the dugout. I was looking at so many things at once that I almost fell down the dugout steps. Luckily, Chief grabbed the back of my shirt with his iron grip and held on until I had my balance.

We walked through the dugout and down a long, cement hallway. We passed the Giants' locker room, the players' voices muffled by a closed door. O'Hara knocked on the next door, and a voice said, "Come in."

He turned the knob and waved us past. A cloud of cigar smoke hung like a curtain in the doorway. It was a small office, most of it filled by a wooden desk. Behind the desk, puffing away, sat John McGraw, still in uniform.

The walls were bare except for two photos. I recognized one right away, the great Christy Mathewson. I leaned toward the wall to read the signature on the other.

"That's Ross Youngs, my right fielder," McGraw said proudly. "If there's a headier ballplayer than him alive, I'd like to meet him."

McGraw turned to Chief. "You look familiar. Do I know you?"

"I tried to introduce myself last night, and you got the law after me," Chief said.

"I remember. You stopped me outside the hotel." McGraw didn't apologize, but he came close. "People come up to me night and day. Either they're a player or someone they know is a player. How was I to know you could throw a ball like that?"

"I told you. I'm the greatest Indian ever gripped a ball."

"What's your name?"

"Chief Sunrise. Are you gonna give me a tryout?"

I was afraid McGraw wouldn't like Chief's attitude, so I dipped my oar in the water.

"He really is great, Mr. McGraw. I'm his catcher."

McGraw looked back and forth from me to Chief. "That must be some league. No offense, son, but you look like a fastball would knock you over. What's your name?"

"Cobb," I answered, my face burning from McGraw's remark. "Hank Cobb."

"You're too small to be a whole cob, son. I'm going to call you Kernel."

McGraw laughed, and O'Hara joined in. I didn't think the nickname was funny. O'Hara must be one of those people who laughs whenever his boss does.

"Go get McCarty," McGraw said when he and O'Hara were done laughing. "Tell him there's someone I want him to catch."

"What if the reporters are still around?" O'Hara asked.

"Unless McCarty's in the saloon across the street, he won't be with the reporters.

"Well, Chief," McGraw announced, pushing back his chair, "let's see if that was a lucky throw or if you really know where the ball is going to end up when you let go of it."

McGraw shoved by us and strode out the door. Chief and I followed. My knees were shaking with excitement. Chief looked calm and confident.

When we reached the field, McCarty was waiting. He looked Chief up and down, spat in the dirt, then pulled on his mask and crouched behind the plate. I imagine he wasn't happy about being called back out to the field after he had squatted for nine tough innings.

McGraw stood behind Chief. O'Hara and I sat on the top step of the dugout. I had my glove out and was pounding my fist into it to hide the fact that my hands were shaking.

"You've got five minutes to show what you've got, Chief. So don't waste time," McGraw barked.

McCarty set up on the edge of the plate, the inside corner to a right-handed batter. Chief wound and fired a fastball that slammed into the catcher's mitt. McCarty moved the target around, but wherever he placed it, Chief hit it.

"Anything besides the fast one?" McGraw asked. His words reminded me of Charlie Conway back at the carnival, only there was a lot more than five dollars at stake this time.

By the time Chief had shown his upshoot and curve ball, McGraw and McCarty were silent. I don't think they could believe their eyes.

Finally McGraw called, "O.K., Lew, you can leave."

McCarty got up and went past me, shaking his head. Just before he left the dugout, McGraw called, "Don't say anything about the Chief here."

McCarty turned and said, "Mr. McGraw, no one would believe me, anyway."

McGraw motioned to Chief, and the two of them came and sat on the bench in the dugout. O'Hara and I turned to face them.

McGraw stared for a moment. Then he said, "How old are you, Chief?"

"Nineteen," Chief answered.

"Where have you played?"

"Here and there."

"That answer is not going to cut it, Chief." McGraw bristled. "This is the big time, New York City. Do you think you can give reporters answers like that?"

Chief shrugged.

"If there's something in your background that you don't want known, tell me about it, and we'll figure out a way to handle the reporters."

"I'm not hidin' anythin'," Chief said, but he didn't look McGraw in the eye when he said it. "I just want to play ball, win some games for the Giants."

McGraw sighed. "The main idea is to win, Chief. You're right on that count."

McGraw turned his attention to O'Hara. "What's the story with the boy?"

"If it wasn't for Hank, we wouldn't have met Chief," O'Hara explained. "Hank talked me into hiring him for the game today."

"Well, Hank, you may be our good-luck charm." McGraw reached over, lifted my ball cap, and rubbed my stubbly head. "A bald head's good luck on a ball club."

I tried not to squirm. This wasn't the time to annoy McGraw.

"I don't want the word to get out," McGraw sighed, "but I'm short of pitchers. Two of my starters, Benton and Toney, are hurting. What would you say to a two-week contract?" he asked Chief. "I'll put you in a game or two and see how you look against a big-league lineup."

"Give me twenty dollars advance," Chief answered, "so Hank and I can get some food and stop dressing like bums, and you've got a deal."

McGraw tilted forward on the bench and pulled his wallet from the rear pocket of his uniform pants. He opened it and peered inside until he found a folded twenty-dollar bill, which he placed in Chief's open palm.

"Spend some of it in the Baths," McGraw said. "There's a good one on Tenth Street and Avenue A.

Ballplayers aren't the cleanest people, but you two have grime ground into you that's got to be steamed out."

Chief and McGraw shook hands.

"Be here at ten tomorrow, and I'll have a contract for you to sign."

He got up to leave, then spoke to me. "How about you, Kernel Hank? How would you like to be combination ball boy and good-luck charm?"

Chief spoke before I could. "Me and Hank are a team. If I'm here, he's here."

"Good. We could use the luck. There was a cross-eyed woman sitting behind first base today, and you saw what happened to Chase. Ordinarily he'd eat up a ground ball like that one."

Following McGraw's advice, we took a streetcar to the steam bath on Tenth Street. Chief paid a dime for each of us, and we walked down a flight of steps into a stone basement. We peeled off our clothes and crammed them into little lockers, hanging the keys around our necks. Then, wrapped in towels, we walked toward the steam room.

I wasn't too happy about wandering around in a strange place wearing nothing but a towel. But Chief was a lot worse off than me. For once it paid to be small. My towel covered everything from my waist down past my knees. The same size towel looked like a diaper on Chief. I followed those enormous legs of his and hoped for the best.

A wave of steam hit us, and I broke into a sweat. We stumbled along, walking toward the heat and the mumble of voices. That steam formed the thickest fog you could imagine, but I kept a death grip on my towel, anyway. If the visibility suddenly improved, I didn't want a bunch of strangers gawking at me.

I could smell my own sweat and wasn't sure how this was supposed to be cleaning me up. Chief felt his way along until his hand found a sort of shelf built into the wall. We boosted ourselves up and sat on it.

After a few minutes, the steam thinned enough for me to make out a bunch of old men, with big bellies and hangy skin, sitting like we were. If these steam baths could make a fellow look like that, we'd have to be careful not to stay too long.

One of the old men slid down and made his way toward a kind of stove in the middle of the room, loose fat jiggling with every step. He dipped a ladle into a bucket and threw water on the stove until the room filled with steam again.

The heat was working its way into my muscles, and surprisingly, it started to feel good. Tight places in my neck and back that I had lived with so long I hadn't realized they were there, relaxed. It left me feeling loose and drowsy.

I must have dozed off, for Chief shook my shoulder and hopped down from the shelf. We felt our way out of the steam room, but turned in the opposite direction of the lockers, our bare feet making little squelchy noises on the cement floor.

The next room was empty except for a row of rusty faucets and a floor that slanted toward a drain in its middle.

Chief turned on a faucet, and water so cold it made my teeth chatter poured down on us. I clamped my jaw and let the drops rattle off me, flushing all that sweat and grime down the drain in the floor.

When we were dressed, we wobbled back onto the street, our legs rubbery from the steam.

"What's next?" I asked Chief.

"First we find a place to get my razor sharpened. Then we buy some clothes that are as clean as we are," Chief said with a grin.

An hour later we were back at our room. We were wearing new clothes and carrying more. From now on, we'd have an extra set just waiting in the room in case we needed them.

Chief dropped his bundle on the bed and pulled out his newly sharpened razor.

"If McGraw thinks a bald head is good luck, we'll keep you smooth as a cue ball," he said. "Take the basin downstairs, and ask them to fill it with hot water. I'll give your head a good shave and sharpen up my Mohawk."

In Uniform

t ten in the morning we were at the players'
entrance to the Polo Grounds. Chief knocked, and
the door was opened by the darkest black man
I'd ever seen.

"Name's Smoky," he announced, "Mr. McGraw's trainer
and clubhouse man. I'm going to fit you gentlemen with
uniforms."

Smoky was the right nickname. His skin was like a
piece of charcoal coated with ash. You had to look past
the top layers to see the black underneath. His head was
covered with thick, gray curls. Smoky sat Chief and me
on a bench in the locker room. He eyeballed our sizes,
unlocked a closet, and started pulling uniforms from its
shelves.

This time I was able to enjoy putting on a uniform, as there wasn't a skirt or bloomer in sight. We dressed in white flannel. The jerseys had New York stitched in orange letters across the chest. Our ball caps and stirrup socks were solid black. Smoky fitted us for baseball shoes. It was the first time I wore a pair of spikes that were the same size as my feet, and I was itching to tear around the bases.

Chief and I would share a locker in a far corner of the room. Smoky brought over gray road uniforms for us to store. Finally, we each got a bulky sweater that buttoned up the front and was also labeled New York. The big leagues were class, no doubt about it.

"Where'd you get a uniform small enough to fit Hank?" Chief asked.

"We've had folks smaller than him with the team," Smoky explained. "The Giants have had all sorts of mascots—dwarfs, hunchbacks. Mr. McGraw's a superstitious man. If he thinks a body's lucky, he sticks with 'em till the luck runs out."

Now I had something else to worry about. If the team went into a slump, McGraw might dump me. I'd have to find some way to make myself useful before that could happen.

"What are the players on this team like?" Chief asked. "Are they friendly?"

"Not to rookies," Smoky answered. "We got a boy named Frisch, runs like the wind, but nobody talks to him."

"Me and Hank'll talk to each other," Chief said. "Anythin' else I should know?"

Smoky looked over his shoulder to make sure the locker room was still empty. "Stay away from Chase," he warned us.

This surprised me. Hal Chase, the smooth first baseman for the Giants, was one of the most popular players in the National League. Everything he did on the field or at bat seemed easy and natural. The reporters called him Prince Hal because the bugs treated him like royalty. I wondered if Smoky knew what he was talking about.

After Smoky's warnings, I thought the Giants might be nasty to us. Instead they acted like we were invisible. When McGraw introduced us, no one even looked up.

Chief disappeared into McGraw's office long enough to sign a contract. Then he jogged in the outfield with the rest of the pitchers. McGraw put a hand on my back and steered me onto the diamond when he went to hit fungoes. My job was to catch the return throws from the fielders and flip the baseballs to him.

McGraw was unbelievable with that fungo bat. He could place the ball wherever he wanted, and he kept the fielders hopping. Most amazing to me was the way he could hit pop-ups straight in the air for the catcher, Lew McCarty, to field. Some of them went so high that McCarty could have refreshed his chaw while he waited for the ball to come down.

During infield practice, the play usually ended at first base, which meant that Hal Chase threw the ball to me. I had the feeling he was trying to make me look bad as he whipped balls into the ground. But I scooped up everything he threw. I hoped that McGraw was noticing what a slick fielder I was.

At last McGraw twirled his fungo bat over his head, signaling the team to come into the dugout. As we trotted off the field it seemed like McGraw pointed the bat at me. The crowd let loose with a roar, and I stuck my chest out and tipped my cap.

The bat boy, a local ten-year-old named Freddy, didn't let me get away with it. "They're cheering the Giants, you jerk, not you," he sneered.

I felt my face flush and said, "Maybe, but someday it will be my turn."

Freddy rolled his eyes. He probably would have given me more lip, but Smoky pointed out the scattered bats and he jumped up to put them in order.

Then it was game time. Sitting on the bench between Smoky and Chief, I couldn't believe my luck. Yesterday I had seen my first big-league game, and today I was in the dugout.

A big right-hander named Fred Toney was the Giants' starting pitcher. Even Chief looked small standing next to him. But Toney wasn't fooling anybody. The Reds teed off on everything he threw, and by the middle of the third inning, the Giants were losing 5–0. The crowd was about half of what it had been on opening day, and if the weather hadn't been so pleasant, some of them might have left. I hoped my good-luck powers weren't being judged by this game.

When the Giants came in to bat in the third, Toney went straight to McGraw. McGraw waved Smoky over, and the two of them held a whispered conference while Toney stretched his arm and made faces. Smoky ran his long fingers up and down the muscles of Toney's right arm, then massaged the elbow. That reminded me that Toney was one of the pitchers McGraw had said was hurting. Suddenly McGraw pointed our way.

"Warm up, Chief. You're going in for Toney," he said.

My heart thrashed around in my chest. Chief spat on the ground, stood, and stretched. A backup catcher named Oil Smith grabbed a mitt. Chief lifted my cap and rubbed my scalp for luck. He and Oil trotted out to the bull pen along the right field line. I couldn't watch him warm up as the bull pen was one of the parts of the field that you couldn't see from the dugout.

My mind was so busy worrying about Chief that I couldn't tell you how the Giants were retired. But the Reds threw their gloves on the ground and ran off the field. Our dugout emptied as the Giants took their defensive positions. Chief walked out to the mound, his eyes focused on the ground as if he were afraid he might trip over the chalk lines.

The bugs buzzed with curiosity. A reporter hung his head down into the dugout and called to McGraw, "Who's the kid?"

"A rookie named Chief Sunrise. Now get out of here," McGraw snapped.

Jake Daubert, a tough lefty, was the first batter Chief would face. McCarty looked into the dugout, and McGraw gave him the sign to relay to Chief. Chief backed Daubert off the plate with a fastball, then struck him out with two curves and an upshoot. I was jumping and hollering, until Smoky pulled me back onto the bench.

"Mr. McGraw don't like too much noise while he's tryin' to think," he mumbled.

Edd Roush was next. The former batting champion hit an easy grounder to Fletcher at short. Greasy Neale followed with a soft fly ball to left, and the side was retired. Chief trotted in, and I met him with my widest grin. He was trying to look like an old pro, taking it all in stride. But his eyes danced with excitement.

The innings went by, and Chief kept abusing the Reds' batters. Oh, they managed a hit or two, but only singles. Meanwhile, the Giants kept scratching at the lead until they trailed by one measly run.

Chase started the Giants' half of the eighth with a single, and McGraw sent the rookie Frisch in to run for him. George Burns, the outfielder who had caught 198 flies last season, was up next. He ripped a single, sending Frisch all the way to third base.

McGraw called, "Kernel Hank, get over here," and I scrambled down to see what he wanted.

He lifted my cap and rubbed my head as McCarty stepped into the batter's box. Lew hit the first pitch right at the shortstop, a sure double play. But the ball skidded through the fielder's legs. Frisch scored and everyone else was safe. McGraw beamed at me, the first time I'd seen him smile other than when he pinned me with my nickname.

"I knew you were lucky, Kernel," he crowed.

McGraw's favorite, Pep Youngs, lined one up the gap in left center. Both runners scored, and the Giants were ahead 7–5. That was the lead Chief went out to protect in the ninth inning. Two pop-ups and a strikeout later, the Giants had won.

Chief shook hands with McCarty, got a pat on the back from Smoky, and was ignored by everyone else. I tried to look calm and professional myself, but a smile so large that the corners of my mouth ached was pasted on my face.

Reading the papers over breakfast the next morning was almost as much fun as being at the ballpark. Not knowing any facts about Chief, the reporters felt free to make things up. They outdid themselves with nicknames.

The *Mirror* called him the "Savage Southpaw" while the *Daily News* went for the "Redman's Revenge." The *Sun* must have noticed his hair style, because they dubbed him the "Mohawk Manipulator." Smoky told us that reporters had come looking for Chief at the Gotham Hotel, but McGraw wouldn't tell them where we were staying.

That day's game was a letdown. Red Causey started for the Giants, and from the way he fared, you'd think his nickname came not from his red hair but from his partiality for the Cincinnati team. I don't think he retired the side in order a single time. Red went the distance but lost badly, 7–2. The game was so one-sided that no one even bothered to rub my head.

The lowly Phillies were the next team to visit the Polo Grounds. An all-day rain washed out Thursday's series opener, which meant that the teams would play two games on Friday. Smoky told Chief that McGraw planned to start him in the second game of the double-header.

Chief and I spent the off day wandering the wet streets, getting to know the city. Going from neighborhood to neighborhood was like visiting different countries. For a while there would be nothing but Italian markets and tenements. Then you'd hit Harlem. One side of the block would be lined with Jewish immigrants wearing prayer shawls. Cross the street, and coloreds were everywhere. The cooking smells drifting out the apartment windows made me think I was back in the Deep South. Whenever our legs got tired, Chief would pull out a couple of nickels, and we'd hop on a streetcar and let it take us wherever it was heading.

We were ambling down 116th Street in a light drizzle when we stumbled upon the Regent Theater.

"Ever been to a motion picture?" Chief asked.

I'd been to nickelodeons a few times, usually when the old man wanted me out of the way so he could shine up to some woman. He always said the best thing about them was the sign on the wall that said Stay as Long as You Like. Once, when I was little, I sat through so many showings of a stagecoach being held up by Indians that I could still run the whole adventure through my mind without missing a detail.

But the nickelodeons had been small and raggedy with shaky camp chairs to sit on. Judging by the size of this place, it might be worth seeing. I looked up at the marquee.

"*Broken Blossoms,*" I groaned. "Sounds like a girlie picture."

Chief pointed at the poster next to the ticket window. It showed one boxer smacking another on the jaw while the beautiful Miss Lillian Gish covered her eyes in fright.

"Looks like a sports picture to me," Chief said. "Let's go."

We paid our dimes and walked into a lobby made from shiny stone. Chief said it was Italian marble, and it had streaks running through it like a cat's-eye I once owned, so he might have been right. The floor was covered with a soft, red rug that reached into every corner of the lobby. A man dressed like a banker out for a night on the town tore our tickets in half, and we walked inside.

Between my gawking and the low lighting, I bumped into the back of a chair. But the chair had so much padding that it didn't hurt. We walked downhill, past hundreds of those padded chairs, all bolted to the floor in curving rows. When we reached the front, we flopped down and sank into that softness.

I leaned back and stared at the stage in front of me. Instead of the movie screen I had expected, there were heavy red curtains with fancy pompoms hanging from the top. I looked up and gasped at the high, curved ceiling. Fancy, gold lights filled with dozens of glass lamps shaped like candles but run by electricity glowed in the dimness. The ceiling itself was painted sky blue. Puffy clouds floated on its surface. It was like being indoors and out at the same time.

There was so much to see that I was almost disappointed when the lights dimmed, the curtains parted to reveal a huge screen, and the show started. But that didn't last for long.

We were sitting close to the piano player, and whatever happened on the screen, he put you right in the mood with his playing. While we watched the boxer train, his hands thumped up and down on that keyboard like the boxer's fists slamming into the heavy bag. But when Miss Lillian Gish, who played the part of the boxer's beautiful daughter, came into view, his fingers tickled the keys ever so softly.

The boxer reminded me a lot of the old man. If he lost a fight or any little thing went wrong, he'd take it out on Miss Lillian Gish, just the way my father would get liquored up and come after me. Each time he hit her, I had to look away from the screen. My eyes flooded with tears, and I was glad Chief was so engrossed in the story that he wasn't paying any mind to me.

For a while, it looked like things were going to work out for Miss Lillian Gish. She ran off from the boxer and met this Chinese man, who hid her and took care of her. He was a bit of an Ethel, sitting around writing poems all the time, but she needed somebody gentle after being used for a punching bag. As the weeks went by they fell in love.

I wish we'd have left right then. If I had known the ending of the picture was going to be so sad, I would have. Some Nosy Parker spots Miss Lillian Gish and tells her father where she's living. He shows up, and when he sees that she's in love with a Chinaman, he goes berserk.

"You're a disgrace to the family!" it says at the bottom of a screen filled with his angry face.

Then, believe it or not, he grabs her by the throat and strangles her. That piano player was banging out deep, sorrowful chords that pressed down like lead weights on my chest.

It was stuffy in the theater, but my skin burst out in goose flesh, and I shook with cold. I swore right then I'd never go back to my old man. If he found me, I'd beg Chief, or John McGraw, or even a cop if I had to, to help me.

I was worried that Chief might think I was a bird for letting a motion picture shake me up, so I tried not to let him get a good look at me when the lights came on. But I think he was as rattled as I was. He kept his face toward the window as we rode the streetcar back to our room. Neither one of us ever mentioned that movie again.

Road Trip

The sun shining in our window woke us up early on Friday morning. Chief and I were ready for a long day at the ballpark. Jesse Barnes pitched the first game of the doubleheader and handled the Phillies easily, 6–2.

Then it was Chief's turn. Early in the game, he relied on his fastball and overpowered the Phillies' anemic lineup. When they started looking for the hot one, McGraw called for breaking pitches. The Phillies were missing so badly that it was painful to watch. Chief's control was deadly, and he shut them out on four hits, the Giants winning 8–0.

This time there was no escaping the reporters as they ambushed Chief at the locker room door. He said as little as possible, leaving them to make up enough to fill their columns. According to which paper you read, Chief was an Apache, a Cherokee, a Seminole, or a Crow. He hailed from Georgia, South Carolina, Florida, or the Midwest. Those reporters never let a lack of information keep them from writing.

Saturday McGraw gave Causey another chance. Red showed he could eat up innings if nothing else. He gave up five runs, but it hardly mattered as the Giants scored thirteen. The Giants had a four and two record, good enough for first place.

Sunday was a travel day for the Giants. Chief and I were told to be at the hotel at seven in the morning to catch a train to Chicago. We'd ride the rails overnight and open a series with the Cubs on Monday afternoon in Weeghman Park.

If there hadn't been much to see on my train ride through the farmlands of the South, this one made up for it. I gawked at cities and towns, bridges and tunnels. Chief buried himself in the sports page of every newspaper he could find, while I read the color comics from each of the cities we passed through. Someone's always laying down a newspaper on a train. All a fellow has to do is be alert to pick it up before the next guy does.

Most of the players napped and talked. Chase walked through the car waving a deck of cards. Zimmerman, the third baseman, center fielder Kauff, and Rube Benton followed him into the dining car for poker. I thought I'd watch the game and see if I could figure out the rules. So I tagged along.

"Beat it, Baldy," snapped Chase. "McGraw won't think

you're so lucky if you're walking around with a size-ten footprint on your rear end."

The rest of the boys laughed like that was the best one they'd ever heard. I left, but I walked real slow so Chase wouldn't think I was scared of him.

Midafternoon Smoky came looking for us. "Mr. McGraw wants to see you," was his brief message.

We followed Smoky through the dining car to McGraw's compartment. Smoky tapped on the door, then led us inside.

"Chief, you pitched a good game yesterday," McGraw greeted him. "The Phillies aren't worldbeaters, but they're big-leaguers and you made them look sad."

"Thanks," Chief mumbled.

"I'd like to change that two-week contract into one for the whole season."

Chief's head snapped up. "Make an offer."

"There's one problem," McGraw said. "I only own a piece of this team. I owe it to my partners to learn more about you first."

Chief sighed. "What is there to know? I've got a fastball, curve, and upshoot. My control's sharp. I don't drink. What's your offer?"

"Where are you from?" McGraw asked.

"Down South in the swamps," Chief snapped.

"What state?"

"How's Florida?"

I could see the color rush to McGraw's cheeks. "Are you from Florida?"

"Sure."

"What part?"

"The swamps, the Everglades."

"Do you have family down there? If you keep pitching like you have been, the reporters will be looking."

"That should keep them busy so they don't bother us."

McGraw glared. "When you're ready to talk honestly, we'll talk contract. You've got eight days to give me some answers, or the Giants will be moving on without you."

Chief turned to leave, and I did, too. But McGraw called me.

"Kernel Hank," he said, "we'll be in Pittsburgh the day Chief's contract runs out. If you decide to stay with the team instead of with Chief, it's all right with me."

Smoky opened the door, and we left. I tried to talk to Chief about why he wouldn't give McGraw more information, but it was like trying to crack a rock with your teeth.

"All he needs to know is I can get people out. If that's not good enough, we'll go elsewhere."

Chief assumed I'd stick with him, even if he left the Giants. Lying awake in an upper berth that night, while Chief contentedly snored in the one below, I realized he was right. Somehow the two of us had become a team.

The Polo Grounds would always be magical to me, the place where the great McGraw had led the Giants to four pennants in the last eight years. Some of the most famous games in baseball history had been played on the site. But the stadium itself was ugly and misshapen with its huge center field and vast foul territory.

Weeghman Park in Chicago was also made of cement, but the place had a softer look. Everything at Weeghman was on a small scale. The fences were close to the plate, and the stands were close to the field.

At the Polo Grounds, if you wanted to watch the game without paying, you had to stand way up on Coogan's Bluff. The players looked like ants. At Weeghman, the park was surrounded by buildings. Folks sat on the rooftops along Waveland Avenue and were no farther from home plate than the bleacher seats were in New York. It seemed to bring the swarming city into the ballpark, or to bring the game out into the city. I was glad we were here for a four-game series. I'd need that long to take it all in.

Freddy was too young to travel with the team, so I would be the bat boy for the road trip. I was glad, because there's only so much you can do as a good-luck charm.

Smoky gave me simple instructions. "Hustle, keep your mouth closed, and keep the bats in good order."

For the opener, McGraw sent Rube Benton to the mound. Rube reminded me of Chief in that he was big and a lefty. But once he let go of the ball, the resemblance ended. Rube threw a soft curve, and his fastball was ordinary. Most times he threw it off the plate as a tease.

Benton was a battler, though, and he pitched out of one jam after another. Several times I braced myself, expecting the Cubs to get that one big hit that would knock the Giants out of the lead. But each time, Benton wiggled out of trouble.

"He bends, but he don't break," was Smoky's opinion.

Luckily the Giants had their hitting shoes on. They battered three Cubs pitchers for eight runs, and we took the game 8–5.

The next day it rained. Chief and I had worked our way through most of that twenty-dollar advance McGraw had given us, and the rest of his salary wasn't due until the end of his two-week contract. So we hung out in the hotel where the team would pay for our meals.

We were both new enough to big-city life that it was fun to sit in the hotel lobby and watch folks pass in and out. Chase and his bunch were locked in a room playing poker, and a few of the other boys were out seeing the sights. But most of the players were content to sit and talk baseball. They didn't exactly include us in the conversation, but they didn't run us off, either. Chief pretended to be reading the sports page, but I think he was listening as closely as I was. If you believed the tales those boys told, it's a wonder they had ever lost a game.

"What was it like playing for Brooklyn and Uncle Robbie?" Pep Youngs asked Lew McCarty. Lew had played for the Robins and their talkative manager, Wilbert Robinson—Uncle Robbie to the bugs.

Lew smiled. "Uncle Robbie was a catcher back in his playing days, and he was always giving us catchers the business. If you made a mistake, all you heard was how sharp he was behind the plate."

"I'll bet that got old fast," Red Causey said with a chuckle.

"It did, but we got him one day," McCarty said.

I could tell from the way Lew settled back in his chair that he was getting ready to spin a good one.

"We were in spring training down in Florida, and a couple of the rookie catchers were having trouble catching foul pops. Uncle Robbie had steam coming out of his ears. 'What difference does it make how high the ball goes?' he asked. 'Why, I could catch a ball dropped off Mount Everest.'"

"Those old-timers can never let anything rest," sighed Art Fletcher.

"Well, the ball club was desperate to draw people and make some money. So the owner hired this girl pilot— Ruth something or other . . ."

"Ruth Law," filled in Fletcher. "I saw her do a loop once that made me sick standing on the ground. That girl is something."

"Right, Ruth Law," went on McCarty. "The ball club hired her to fly over the field and do some stunts before the games. Well, I don't know what gave me the idea, but I challenged Uncle Robbie to catch a ball dropped from her plane—just to show the rookies how easy those high pops were."

"Did he try it?" I couldn't help but blurt.

"I could tell he wanted to back out," McCarty said, ignoring me, "but the players and a couple of sportswriters were eyeballing him, so he said, 'If she can drop it on the infield, I'll catch it.'

"The writers put it in the papers, so next day there's a big crowd at the ballpark. Uncle Robbie, looking kind of green around the gills, is standing at home plate wearing his old, beat-up catcher's mitt, while this airplane circles over the field. Suddenly, he stiffens up and starts waddling back and forth between home plate and the pitcher's mound. The crowd lets out this godawful roar as they spot something falling from the sky. I'll be darned if that fat, old man didn't settle right under that thing and hold up his glove proud as you please."

"Did he catch it?" Youngs asked.

"It burst right through his glove, and a wet liquid sprayed all over him. Uncle Robbie fell flat on his back, yelling, 'Help me, lads. I'm covered with my own blood!' The crowd fell silent. We all rushed out to him. I was one of the first ones there, and I could see right away that he wasn't bleeding."

"What was it?" Fletcher wondered.

"That fool girl had taken off without the baseball. She knew she had to drop something, so she fished a grapefruit out of her lunch and pitched that out the window."

I laughed so hard that my ribs ached. Chief kept the sports page in front of his face, but I could tell from the way the pages rattled that he was laughing, too.

Smoky came looking for us after lunch. "Mr. McGraw wants to know, how's your arm?" he said.

"Good," was Chief's reply.

"Rain means we play two tomorrow. You'll be startin' the second game."

Chief nodded and went back to his newspaper. I was glad everyone on the team wasn't as quiet as Chief. It would make for some long afternoons.

Double Duty

eeghman Park looked greener than ever after the daylong rain. The air had that rich spring-time smell of things growing, and the ballplayers had an extra bounce in their stride after the day of rest.

Smoky had been working on Toney's arm all week, and he was going to test it out in game one. The Giants scored a couple of runs in the first inning. Since the Cubs' nickname was the "hitless wonders," I was feeling pretty good.

But Toney gave those two runs back fast. His pitches were slow and straight. When former Giant "Bonehead" Merkle singled to tie the score, Toney hadn't retired a single batter. McGraw told Chief to warm up and went out to the mound to stall for time. Chief and Oil Smith hustled out to the bull pen while McGraw jawed with Toney.

Before long, the umpire yelled for McGraw to get off the field. McGraw used that opportunity to start an argument that bought Chief another couple of minutes. Just when the ump was about to throw him out of the game, McGraw signaled for Chief to take over on the mound. By that time Chief's arm was loose, and he was ready to go.

Merkle had been on first base for so long that you could hardly blame him for not being alert. Chief picked him off before he threw a pitch. Then he struck out two batters to get out of the inning.

The Giants had plenty of base runners, but couldn't squeeze a run across the plate against the Cubs' ace, Hippo Vaughn. Chief held the Cubs scoreless, and the game was still tied in the ninth inning.

Chief was the first batter up. He swung like he was trying to fight off a hornet with the bat, but he got enough of the ball to bloop it over the shortstop's head for a single.

Burns was next. He ran his hand up and down the barrel of his bat as he stepped into the batter's box. That was his signal for the hit-and-run. Chief took off, and Burns hit a hard ground ball right back to the pitcher. Vaughn whirled and threw to second to start a double play. Chief slid high and hard, knocking the second baseman over before he could throw the ball. Chief was out at second, but Burns was safe. When Youngs hit one up the gap, the lead run scored. Chief mowed the Cubs down in the ninth, and the Giants had the win.

Smoky came over to congratulate Chief in the locker room between games.

"Who's pitchin' game two?" Chief asked.

"That's what McGraw's tryin' to figure out," Smoky answered. "Barnes will be ready tomorrow, but his arm tightens up if he tries to go on short rest."

Chief crossed the room and rapped on McGraw's door. He came out smiling a minute later.

"What's up?" I asked, since Chief wasn't big in the smile department.

"McGraw's lettin' me pitch the second game, too."

Chief started great, then hung on gamely to the finish. The Giants were finding those short outfield fences at Weeghman an easier target than the Cubs were. They put nine runs up on the scoreboard, and that was more than enough. The Cubs got four off Chief, all in the last three innings.

When the game ended and the disappointed Cubs fans were filing out of the park, Chief got pats on the back from most all his new teammates. Pitching eighteen innings in one day had earned the respect of the veterans.

Only Chase had something ornery to say. "When your arm falls off, you'll be sweeping the streets for nickels while McGraw is still living high. Wise up, rookie."

Chase started me wondering. Chief had only five days left on his contract. Suppose he developed a sore arm and McGraw cut him loose. What would happen to us then?

I guess the Giants used up all their hitting in the doubleheader. The next day Barnes pitched a good ball game, but the Cubs nipped him 2-1. My head got a workout in the ninth inning with every batter giving it a rub. It seemed like my good-luck powers were working as we scored a run and loaded the bases with one out. Then Zimmerman ripped a ball over the bag at third that looked like a gamer. Somehow, the Cubs' third sacker, a stiff named Charlie Deal, picked it clean. He stepped on third and fired a strike to first for the double play that ended the game.

Chase made me feel bad by sneering, "Looks like you're Deal's good-luck charm today, Kernel."

I'd gotten used to McGraw calling me Kernel. He treated me good and always let me field for him when he hit fungoes. But Chase said the nickname with such poison in his voice that it made me feel undersized and hopeless.

The loss made the train ride to St. Louis a quiet one. I was as nervous as a tightrope walker with athlete's foot. Chief's contract was about to expire, and he was no more willing to tell McGraw about his past than he had ever been. We crossed paths with McGraw in the dining car, and he just nodded and went about his business.

We ate a late dinner on the train, then headed for bed. I climbed into a top berth, while Chief slid into the one underneath. While I tossed and turned, he snored loud enough to warn wildlife to clear the tracks.

After a big breakfast in the dining car, we rode a streetcar from the station to the ballpark. I got my first peek at the mighty Mississippi, sluggish, brown, and filled with floating debris, but my mind was on baseball. Today I'd see the great Rogers Hornsby, and I couldn't wait.

I was hoping for a chance to ask him if he really had played for the Bloomers. As it turned out, I didn't get to talk to him personally, but I saw more of Hornsby than I wanted. Benton pitched for the Giants, and again he had nothing. He tried floating those curve balls of his past Hornsby, and he didn't have a chance. The Rajah smacked three doubles and a single, and the Cards won 7–3.

This was the first time the Giants had lost two in a row. With a 7 and 4 record we trailed the Reds by one game. The Cincinnati team had been going strong ever since leaving New York.

Between the travel and the ball game, it figured to be an early night. McGraw stood in the hotel dining room and warned everyone that Smoky would be around at ten o'clock to do a bed check. Anyone who wasn't in his room would be fined. Then he added something I didn't expect.

"And if you do go out tonight, stay away from East St. Louis. There's trouble there that doesn't concern anyone on this ball club. You can throw your money away in the bars on this side of the Mississippi without getting a lump on your head for thanks."

After dinner, I picked up a copy of the *St. Louis Post-Dispatch* that someone had left in the lobby. There was the headline: "Three Dead in Riot."

I looked for Chief, but he had his head buried in the *Sporting News*. Not that it mattered. I could guess that his reaction would be no reaction. The story said that a gang of unemployed whites, mostly soldiers back from the war, had attacked a Negro work crew coming out of a factory. The coloreds took the worst of it, being unarmed and surprised. They'd been striking back, though, jumping any whites who came through their neighborhood. No wonder McGraw didn't want his players wandering over there.

When Smoky peeked in for bed check, Chief was asleep, and I was reading the *Sporting News*, checking the minor-league rosters for any name that might belong to my old man. Things had looked bad for him when he fell off the train, but I had seen him talk his way out of some dire situations.

I searched for players with the initials H. B., since the old man always stuck with that combination, no matter how many times he changed his name. You'd think he had monogrammed hankies or something. The only H. B. I found was the bat company, Hillerich and Bradsby. Maybe the old man really was out of circulation this time.

Chief was trimming the edges of his Mohawk next morning when Smoky knocked and stuck his head in the door.

"Chief, stop up to Mr. McGraw's room before you go to breakfast."

I followed Chief to the elevator, and we rode up to the third floor. I paced back and forth in the car, knowing our fate was about to be decided. Chief leaned against the wall and yawned.

McGraw's door was open. He sat in an easy chair, puffing a cigar and reading the newspaper. Chief rapped on the open door, and McGraw set the paper down.

"Chief, you showed me something pitching that doubleheader in Chicago," McGraw began. "You were willing to risk your arm for the team, even though you knew your contract would run out in a few days."

"I came here to play ball, not to watch," Chief said with a shrug.

"You took a chance, and now I'm going to take one." McGraw reached into his jacket pocket and pulled out a folded set of papers. "Sign on the dotted line, Chief, and you're a Giant for the rest of the season."

I felt like jumping in the air, but instead slid behind Chief so my excitement wouldn't show.

"What's the pay?" Chief asked.

"Rookies usually get two thousand dollars," McGraw said. "I'm giving you two thousand on top of the two-weeks' pay you've already earned."

Chief nodded and reached for a pen that lay on the table next to McGraw's chair. He signed his name, and they shook hands.

"Take care of yourself, and work hard. Maybe there will be a World Series check this fall," McGraw said.

"You won't be sorry, Mr. McGraw," Chief promised.

Night Shift

C hief got plenty of work. Fred Toney was sent back to New York to have his pitching arm examined. The doctor advised him to rest for at least a month. Benton claimed that his arm felt fine, but he tired after pitching two or three innings. So the rotation was Barnes, Chief, and Causey, or just Barnes and Chief when the schedule was light.

The Giants continued the road trip, playing series in Pittsburgh, Philadelphia, and Boston. Chief won in all three cities, giving him seven wins without a loss. His winning streak ended in Brooklyn. Spitballer Burleigh Grimes nipped Chief 2–1.

The games in Brooklyn counted as part of our road trip, but Ebbets Field was so close to the Polo Grounds that we lived the same as if we were playing at home.

Now that Chief was signed up for the season, he and I moved out of our little room over the saloon and into the Gotham Hotel with McGraw and the single players.

My head was spinning from all that I'd seen. In a few short weeks, I'd visited five cities besides New York and been in uniform in seven different stadiums. Now I had faces to match with the names of the National League stars my old man had talked about for so long. I had watched Rogers Hornsby lash a double with a flick of his powerful wrists. I had seen Grover Cleveland Alexander stare at a batter until his knees shook. My old life seemed strange and distant, like something that had happened to another person.

Lots of players, Hal Chase for one, were squawking that they were underpaid. They claimed that the owners made huge profits and gave them peanuts. But for me and Chief, two thousand dollars seemed like all the money in the world. For us it was a novelty to have three meals a day, plenty of clothes, and a clean place to sleep.

The Giants entered a three-week stretch of home games. The schedule was a breeze without travel mixed in. The team played a game every afternoon except Sunday. Sunday baseball was illegal in New York, unless the bugs were let in for free, and the owners weren't likely to let that happen.

Chief and I would get up every morning and have a big breakfast in the hotel while we caught up on the sports page. Then we'd stroll down to the Polo Grounds and put on our uniforms. We were usually the first ones there, so we'd have time for a catch.

Sometimes Chief would pitch me batting practice. I can't describe what it felt like to stand up at the plate in a big-league stadium. Most days I couldn't stop smiling.

When the other players arrived, I'd stick with McGraw, running errands and handling the throws while he hit fungoes. The longer I was with the team, the more chores McGraw found for me to do. It seemed like whenever he was in the dugout or on the field, he wanted me by his side. That was fine with me. I figured that a kid like me couldn't hang around McGraw without learning the game, no matter how dumb he was.

I asked Smoky once why McGraw wanted me around so much. I wasn't complaining, but it had been my experience that grownups thought of young guys like me as pests. I was used to men treating me the way Chase did.

"Managing is lonely work, Kernel Hank," Smoky said, rubbing a hand through his gray tangle of hair. "McGraw can't get friendly with the players, or they'll try to take advantage. That leaves me, you, and Freddy to choose from. And you know how aggravational Freddy can be."

Freddy was kind of thick. He couldn't learn the simplest things, like keeping the bats in a neat row. McGraw told him a dozen times that crossed bats were bad luck, but at least once a game, Freddy would lay them down that way. When Chase ended a rally by striking out with the bases loaded using a crossed bat, Freddy was through. That made me full-time bat boy.

Every night Chief and I would walk around town after dinner. Sometimes we'd visit a nickelodeon, but mostly we were happy to wander the streets and watch people. Neither one of us suggested going back to the Regent or trying any of the other theaters. *Broken Blossoms* had left us with a bad feeling about motion pictures. Bed check was ten o'clock, and we were ready for sleep by the time Smoky stuck his head in to make sure we were in our room.

One night, I couldn't stomach dinner in the hotel. It was fish, and the smell alone was too much for me. So when we were on our walk, I wolfed down a couple of greasy sausages that I bought on the street. I woke up in the middle of the night with my stomach turning somersaults. Bent over, I stumbled across the room and down the hall to the toilet.

What happened in there is better left unsaid. In about ten minutes I felt weak, but halfway human again. I made my way back to our room and cracked the door open as quietly as I could. I got back to bed, feeling proud of myself that I hadn't woken Chief. Then I noticed the stillness. I'd been sleeping in the same room with Chief for more than a month, and he was not a peaceful sleeper. Chief snored, and that noise was drowned out every couple of minutes by urgent messages from his stomach to the outside world.

I was thinking of calling Chief's name or getting up and going over to his bed, when I heard a creaking sound. The door to our room opened. Chief tiptoed in, carrying the new shoes he had bought with part of his first paycheck. He closed the door with barely a click from the latch. The room was pitch dark, but I could hear him walk over to his bed and get undressed. I didn't smell any booze, and he wasn't banging into things, so I knew he hadn't been drinking. Where had he wandered off to in the middle of the night?

Come morning, Chief acted the same as always. He didn't mention sneaking out, and I didn't bring it up, either. Whatever he had been up to didn't affect his pitching. Chief shut out the Pirates on five hits in front of a big Saturday crowd.

The locker room emptied quicker than usual after the game. The reporters were so anxious to file their stories and start their weekend that they forgot to pester Chief with personal questions. Players scattered to enjoy the city. Tonight there would be no bed check, since Sunday was an off day.

Chief and I went for our regular ramble after dinner and then up to our room. I pretended I was tired and went to bed as early as I dared without making Chief suspicious. Then came the hard part. I had to lie still without falling asleep. Every few minutes I'd open my eyes a slit, but whenever I peeked, Chief was sitting up in bed reading the *Sporting News*.

I must have dozed off, because a sharp click jerked me awake. I sat up to a dark room, sure that Chief was sneaking out. I jumped out of bed and pulled on my pants and shirt. I forced my feet into my shoes. My Giants sweater was at the foot of the bed, and I stuck my arms into the sleeves as I opened the door. The hallway was empty, but I could hear footsteps going down the fire stairs. By the time I reached the top of the stairs, the fire door was closing down below.

I bent to tie my shoes, then raced for the main staircase. I tore down the steps and through the lobby. If McGraw or Smoky had been there, I'd have faced a million questions. But no one was around, so I was out the door and sprinting for the corner. Once there, I turned left and ran for a block.

Now I was behind the hotel. If Chief had come out the alley that led from the fire door, he had to be on this street. At first I thought I had missed him, but then I saw a tall figure pass under the streetlight and turn the corner a block north of where I stood. I raced after him.

At the end of the block, I leaned against a building to catch my breath and peeked around the corner. Chief was a half block ahead. I stayed where I was until he had a full-block lead, then took off after him again.

Careful to lay back and stay in the shadows, I followed Chief through the colored neighborhoods of Harlem. Since it was Saturday night, there were lots of people on the streets, many in fancy clothes. Mine wasn't the only white face, but there were an awful lot of dark ones. I wasn't afraid, though, as no one seemed to be paying any attention to me.

The music of trumpets and drums leaked from the bars and clubs that lined the street on both sides. I might have lost Chief if he hadn't been so tall that his head stuck up above the crowd. Still, I tried to close the gap between us.

I was hustling around a gang of coloreds, all decked out in their Saturday finest, and almost ran into Chief's back. He had stopped at the entrance to a club called

Harlem Hotspot and was talking to the man guarding the door. I ducked behind a sandwich board advertising the group playing the club, the Fabulous Coal Brothers. A piano was tinkling away inside, and drums beat a rhythm I could feel in my belly.

The man left the entrance, and Chief turned, as if to read the sandwich board that hid me. I thought I was nailed, but another bunch of Negroes showed up and crowded in between us. Chief turned and stared out into the street.

After a few minutes, the man returned and led Chief inside. "Mr. Foster will see you now," he said.

Chief followed him into the Hotspot. I hung around for a while, racking my brain for any Mr. Foster that Chief might have mentioned. Who could he be? And why had Chief snuck out of the hotel to see him? It was Saturday night. He was free to come and go as he pleased.

There was a long line of people waiting for a chance to get into the club, and pretty soon a party had started in the street. Couples danced to the tunes seeping through the door of the nightclub and passed flasks back and forth. A long, black car cruised up to the curb, and the crowd buzzed with excitement. What was the thrill in watching a bunch of rich folks walk past you and enter a club that you'd been waiting an hour or more to get into?

I was about to go back to the hotel when Chief came out the door. He stuffed his hands in his pockets and walked off, eyes fixed on the sidewalk. He passed within five feet of me, but never saw me. I followed cautiously for the first couple of blocks. Then, when I was sure he was heading for the Gotham, I took off at a dead run. I circled around Chief's route and came at the hotel from the far side. Peeking around the corner, I didn't see Chief, so I hurried through the front door and up to our room.

I stripped down to my skivvies and jumped into bed. By the time my breathing had slowed to normal, I heard Chief creeping in. Within minutes, he was playing his nighttime symphony of snores. But I lay awake for a long time asking myself what he had been up to.

I stayed awake as late as I could every night for the next week, but Chief didn't sneak out again. His goal must have been to meet with that Mr. Foster, whoever he was, and he had done that. When McGraw caught me yawning in the dugout and asked if I was getting bored with the big leagues, I decided to give up my night watchman's job and concentrate on being a good bat boy.

The Team That
Never Traveled

S pring stretched into summer. The days were so
long that even extra-inning games ended in broad
daylight. Road and home series followed each
other in an endless loop. Chief and Jesse Barnes were
having great seasons. They kept the Giants in the pen-
nant race. The rest of the pitching staff was a shambles.

Fred Toney never recovered. Twice he rejoined the
team and tried to pitch, but each time he threw a few
good innings only to have his arm tighten up. Slowly but
surely the Reds were pulling away. They led by three
games in June, five by Fourth of July, and seven on
August first.

It was then that we got invited to the prison. The
team had dropped a Monday afternoon game to the Cubs
when Zimmerman booted a grounder with the bases

loaded. He and Chase were in a foul mood in the club-house, and I was trying to stay away from them.

McGraw stuck his head in the door and said, "Don't make any plans for Sunday, men. We're playing an exhibition game in Ossining."

"Ossining?" Chase blurted. "We're major-leaguers. Why do we have to go play in the sticks? Can't the team at least come here?"

McGraw smiled and said, "You might like to play for this team, Chase. They play all their games at home. Bus leaves at 10 A.M., Sunday."

Zimmerman said, "That's what's wrong with this team. Instead of getting our rest, we have to go on a Sunday road trip. What's so special about these guys that they can't travel?"

Smoky looked up from the bench where he was stuffing dirty uniforms into a laundry bag. "These boys are locked in," he said. "We're going to Sing Sing."

Sing Sing! What boy could hear the name without a delicious chill of fear shooting up his spine? Hadn't I read a feature article in the *Police Gazette* about the famous prison?

The most notorious criminals in New York State ended up in Sing Sing, and the worst of those finished their days strapped into "Old Sparky," the inmates' nickname for the electric chair. Back in 1912, seven prisoners had been executed on the same day. My old man claimed that all the lights in New York City flickered each time some desperado got fried.

According to Smoky, the warden of Sing Sing was a baseball fanatic. He'd noticed that some of the prisoners playing ball in the yard had talent. Figuring baseball would be a great way to keep the men busy, he encouraged them to compete among themselves. Before long, each cellblock had its own team.

The warden's next idea was to form an all-star team and challenge the major-league squads in the area. Already the prisoners had played the Robins and the Yankees. Now it was our turn.

Sunday morning, in full uniform, we left the team bus and boarded a ferry for our ride "up the river" to Sing Sing. Chief and I stood at the rail, a stiff breeze trying to tear our caps from our heads. The Hudson River was alive with wheeling birds and boats of all shapes and sizes.

A bus from the prison met us at the Ossining landing. We filed on board, Chase and Zimmerman still grousing about losing a day off. McGraw ignored them and sat silently in the front seat with Smoky by his side.

The bus wound through narrow streets until we came to the twenty-foot stone walls of the famous prison. The driver let us off by the main gate where the warden was waiting. He shook hands with McGraw and led us inside the compound.

Crossing the exercise yard, I stared up at the bleak, gray walls. Armed guards called down to us from their posts in towers spaced every few feet along the walls. We rounded a corner of the main building and came upon a half circle of men in identical gray shirts and pants, all with their hair cut short. They sat on the grass, ringing the outfield. Guards led us to a path left open between those prisoners and hundreds more who filled the bleachers.

I kept my eyes straight ahead. I was scared stiff and didn't want the convicts to see it. Cheers and catcalls poured down from the bleachers and up from the players seated on the ground.

McGraw said, "Your diamond's in great shape, Warden. The turf is equal to that at the Polo Grounds."

"Thank you, Mr. McGraw," the warden answered. "I've got plenty of man power. This field keeps a whole crew busy." I could tell from his face that the diamond was his pride and joy.

I couldn't wait to duck into the dugout, out of sight of those staring convicts. Only there were no dugouts. The Giants would sit in a row of folding chairs between the first baseline and one set of bleachers. The Sing Sing nine would occupy the same setup on the third base side of the field.

We had just gotten seated and were watching the convicts take infield practice when a ball sailed over the first baseman's head. I jumped up and snagged it on one bounce. The first baseman turned toward me to take my throw. I pulled back my arm and froze.

The first baseman was my old man.

For a second his surprise showed equal to mine. Then those eyes of his burned into me, and he said, "Did you forget how to throw a ball, Hank?"

I whipped the ball at his head with all my might. He flicked his glove and caught it effortlessly. Then he turned to his teammates and got back to work.

I stood frozen until Chief grabbed my arm and led me to a chair.

"What is it, Hank? Do you know that guy?" he asked.

"He's my father," I whispered.

I was stunned. Instead of spreading the bats in a neat row, I left them packed in their canvas sack. Smoky asked what was wrong, and after a huddled conference with Chief, he spread the news to McGraw. McGraw eyeballed me, but he didn't come over.

Chief ended up playing first base for the Giants that day. Chase claimed he had a tender ankle, so McGraw left him out of the lineup. I overheard him telling Zimmerman his real reason for begging off. "I don't play against coloreds. It ain't natural."

I had been in such a daze that I hadn't noticed my old man's teammates. The catcher, the second baseman, and one of the outfielders were colored. It was the first time I had ever seen a mixed-race team.

Benton pitched for the Giants, and his assortment of junk was more than the convicts, colored or white, could handle. The hitters who had been slamming the ball in batting practice looked helpless against major-league pitching.

The crowd was noisy, but the bugs' remarks were no nastier than what flew out of the stands in Brooklyn when we were giving their beloved Robins a whipping. When they were cheering, they sounded like any other crowd.

The old man was as tough an out as ever. He let Benton's wild ones go by, trying to force him to throw a fastball. The first two times he was up, Benton hit the corners and got the old man to ground out. But the third time, Benton fell behind three balls and a strike. When he threw the straight one, the old man was ready. He lined it over third for a double.

All I wanted was for the game to end so I could get out of there. My mind spun with a million questions. How had the old man ended up in a New York prison when I'd seen him get nabbed in Georgia? How long was his sentence? What would I do now that he knew where to find me?

By the time the last of the convicts had grounded out to the old man's hero, Artie Fletcher, I had the bats packed. While the players were shaking hands I tried to get Smoky moving toward the gate. But he took the sack of bats off my shoulder and laid it on the ground.

"We stay here until they march these convicts back to their cellblocks," he said and flopped down on one of the folding chairs.

I might have to wait, but I couldn't sit. I paced back and forth. McGraw was talking to the warden, who had acted as manager for the inmates' squad. The warden spoke. McGraw looked my way and nodded his head. He called Chief over, and the three of them held a conference.

Smoky said, "Looks like they talkin' about you, Kernel Hank."

McGraw and Chief walked toward me while the warden gathered his team.

"Kernel Hank," McGraw began, "your father wants to talk to you."

"Suppose I don't want to talk to him?" I said and spat on the ground.

"It's your choice," McGraw said, "but I think you should. He can make trouble for Chief and the ball club. He says we've got no right to have you with us. He's asking if you went to school this spring."

My face flushed with anger. When we were together, the old man had never worried about school. "He's just saying that to get after me," I complained.

"Why not talk to him?" McGraw urged. "Introduce him to Chief. Show him you're in good hands."

Chief put an arm on my shoulder and said, "It's safe, Hank. I'll be with you, and a guard will be standing a few feet away."

"All right," I said, "but if you think he's worried about me, you're wrong. He never cared about anyone but himself in his whole life."

Chief and I stood and waited while McGraw talked to the warden. I tried not to think about poor Miss Lillian Gish with that boxer's big paws wrapped around her neck.

All this time the bleachers and grounds had been emptying of convicts. The rest of the prison team had left the field, but the old man stood near the pitcher's mound, his cap held in front of him, and a guard nearby.

McGraw and the warden shook hands. The rest of the Giants followed him around the corner of the main building and out of sight. The old man walked toward me. I fought to look him in the eye, but my head slowly lowered until I was staring at the grass. When I could see his battered spikes in front of me, he spoke.

"Hello, Hank. How've you been?"

Tears welled in my eyes. My old man didn't care about me. Why was he pretending to now?

"I'm good," I managed to say.

"Don't you want to ask how I am?" was the old man's next question.

My head snapped up, anger replacing the hurt and fear. The questions poured out of me.

"How'd you get here? Why were those men chasing you down in Georgia? Why are you making believe to care about me?"

The old man smiled. He turned to Chief and said, "Does he get mouthy with you like that, too?"

Chief gave him the deadpan stare, so the old man turned back to me.

"All right, Hank, here's the story. I was lifting a wallet off a drunk when all hell broke loose. An old biddy spotted me and yelled bloody murder. Turns out the drunk was some kind of war hero, so before I knew it, half the town was chasing me. When I didn't make it onto the train, I ended up in jail."

I looked at him then to see how mad he was about my letting him fall.

"You did the right thing, Hank," he surprised me by saying. "That's the first time I knew you'd been listening to the lessons I taught you. If I wasn't strong enough to get on that train by myself, that was my problem. Try to help the other guy and you might lose your own freedom. When you let me go, I thought there was hope for you yet."

Chief couldn't let that one pass. "Hank and I got to the big leagues by helpin' each other," he said, glaring at the old man.

"I'll get to you in a minute," the old man said. "I'm not done talking to my boy.

"So I was rotting in a cell in Georgia, three years for assault and robbery. Then the guards want to know if anyone can play baseball. Sing Sing Prison is looking for players. The warden thinks he can build a team that can compete with the big-leaguers. I know that's nonsense, but what do I care? They run me through my paces, and I'm in. I had a fine train ride from Georgia to New York, good grub all the way. I play ball every day. It's better than sitting in a cell. And now, I've found my boy besides."

"Like you care," I couldn't help saying.

"Be sassy as you like, Hank. I'll get out of here someday, and then I'll remind you how to speak to your pa."

He smiled when he said it to keep the guard happy.

"Now I'm ready to talk to you, Charlie," he said to Chief.

"His name's not Charlie," I said, but the sick expression on Chief's face stopped me cold.

"Sure it is," said the old man with a grin. "Charlie Dawn. One of the boys on our team played ball with him out in Indiana."

"There's no law against taking a new name," I argued, "or you'd have a life sentence."

138

"That's true, Hank, unless you have a reason for hiding your identity."

Chief's face was darker than I'd ever seen it. The jagged, pink line of his scar pulsed in his cheek.

"Charlie, you were bragging how you and my boy helped each other. Now the two of you are going to help me. Are you pitching against Brooklyn tomorrow?"

"Tuesday," Chief answered.

"Well, I hate to break it to you, Charlie, but you're going to get hammered. Brooklyn's going to win that ball game."

I was expecting Chief to laugh in his face or tell him where to go. Instead he said, "What happens if they don't?"

"To start with, Charlie, your face is on the front page of every newspaper in New York come Wednesday morning. You'll never pitch in the big leagues again."

"I guess I've got no choice." Chief sighed.

My mouth was hanging open so wide that I could have swallowed a baseball if one had come sailing our way.

"One more thing," the old man said. "I want Hank to start visiting me on Sundays whenever the Giants are in town. He'll tell you which other games you're going to lose. Visiting hours are noon to two."

The old man stuck out his hand for Chief to shake. Chief glared, wrapped an arm around my shoulder, and led me toward the gate.

Charlie Dawn's Story

On the way up the river, I hadn't been able to take my eyes off the water. Now I might as well have been closed up in a windowless boxcar. Chief and I were standing alone at the rail, but I was blind to my surroundings.

"I'm not an Indian, Hank," was his opener.

"Why did you say you were?" I asked.

"To explain my dark skin," Chief said.

Then it hit me. He was colored. I thought of the fighting going on between whites and blacks. The riots in East St. Louis and Washington. What would people do if they found out they'd been rooting for a colored man all summer long without even knowing it?

"Your skin's not that dark," I said, still hoping it wasn't true.

"My pa is white, but in this country, if you're part colored, you're all colored."

"Is that why you snuck off into Harlem to meet that Mr. Foster?"

Now it was Chief's turn to look shocked. "How'd you know about Rube Foster?"

"I followed you."

"Rube Foster's got nothin' to do with me bein' on the Giants. That was my idea. He's startin' his own league next year, the Negro National League, and I'm goin' to be part of it."

"If you don't get killed first," I said. "Why'd you pull this stunt—for the money?"

"No, Hank. I did it for me."

"What do you mean?"

"I had to prove to myself that I could play with anybody. My pitchin's just as tough for a white man to hit as a Negro. I've beaten every team in the league except Brooklyn, and I'm goin' to whip them on Tuesday. No matter how many years it is before they let colored in the majors, I'll know I was good enough to be there all along."

"If you don't lose that game, the old man will rat you out. Believe me, he's got no conscience," I said. "Besides, won't the gamblers be after you?"

"I've got two days to figure somethin' out, Hank. All's I know right now is that I'm goin' to win that game."

We were quiet for a while, staring at the point where the ferry cut through the current.

"Suppose the story does break," I said at last. "Haven't you proven that colored can play in the big leagues?"

"People will say the games were fixed or come up with some other excuse. Besides, Rube Foster's got a better plan."

"What is it?"

"Who do you think colored bugs would rather see play—Negroes or whites? He figures to put a team in every city with a large Negro population. When he steals all those bugs from the white clubs, what will the owners do?"

"I don't know, cut expenses somehow."

"They'll cut salaries, Hank. They always do when times are tough. There's dozens of stars like Chase already complainin' that they're bein' robbed blind by the owners. They'll go where the money is. Before you know it, there'll be whites tryin' to get in our league. Once that happens, mixed teams will start poppin' up everywhere, even in the majors."

"Then why not leave now? If you don't pitch at all on Tuesday, you can't be expected to throw the game."

"I won't be satisfied till I beat every team in the league, and I've got one more to go."

I never should have read the papers Monday morning, for they only made me more nervous. While the Giants had been facing the Sing Sing nine, a huge march called the "Silent Parade" had been held in Harlem. The papers reported that thousands of Negroes had marched through the streets in total silence. They carried signs demanding the fair treatment that the laws of the United States promised them. Who would think that the best way to be heard was to stay quiet?

The whole thing had come off peacefully, but everyone from the desk clerk at the hotel to the shop owners on our block were saying how the coloreds were getting out of line. Why did bad feelings have to be at their peak just when Chief was in danger of being exposed?

Every time a teammate approached Chief, I thought he had discovered his secret and was going to call him on it. I remembered how mad the fans had gotten at "Janet" Jameson when he had pretended to be a girl. People didn't like to be made fools of, and any way you looked at it, that's what Chief had done.

If Chief was nervous, it didn't show. He ran his laps, threw on the sidelines, and soaked up every detail of the game, same as always. If I'd been him, I think I'd have turned white out of fear. I know Brooklyn won the game 6–2, but I might as well have been back in the hotel for all I saw of it.

Monday night I tossed and turned while Chief snored. Finally, I gave up trying to sleep and passed the night studying batting averages in the *Sporting News*. When the sun came up, I was there to greet it.

Chief had his usual appetite at breakfast. Pitching or not, he could put away eggs, flapjacks, and half a hog's worth of bacon in that hotel dining room. I choked down a little toast and some coffee.

We walked to the ballpark in silence. If Chief went ahead and won today, I was sure the old man would expose him. If he lost, the old man would never let him off the hook. Chief and I loved baseball more than anything, and we'd be forced to help the old man fix games.

Somehow the hands crawled around the clock face and reached game time. One thought made me feel better. Chief might try his best and still lose. The Robins were pitching their spitballing veteran, Burleigh Grimes. The Giants never had much success against him. Then I realized that the old man had done it again. He had me rooting against my best friend, and my own team.

Chief blew away all three batters in the first inning. The Giants threatened in their half, loading the bases with two outs. Then Chase whiffed, waving at a spitter that dove into the dirt.

The game stayed scoreless into the seventh inning. Brooklyn had two runners on with one out when Zach Wheat hit a double play ball to Doyle on second. Doyle flipped it to Fletcher. Fletcher stepped on second base and gunned the ball waist high to Chase at first. Chase dropped the ball.

Chief had run over to back up first base, and he glared menacingly at Chase. Chase ignored him and went to work smoothing out the dirt around the bag with his spikes.

Hy Myers was the next batter for the Robins. Hy hit a dribbler down the first baseline. Chief was off the mound like a cat. He grabbed the ball, but instead of throwing it to Chase, he raced Myers to the bag.

Chase never moved. There was a three-way pileup as Chief and Myers reached the bag and crashed into him.

The umpire snapped his right fist in the air and yelled, "Out!" loud enough for everyone in the stadium to hear.

Chief regained his feet by doing a push-up on Chase's chest and ran into the dugout. Chase took his time getting up and brushed himself off before leaving the field. In the dugout, he looked at Chief with such hatred in his eyes that I thought there would be a fight. But McGraw stepped between them.

"He showed me up," Chase snarled, waving his arm at Chief.

"I wasn't givin' you another chance to keep that innin' alive," Chief said. He shoved past Chase and picked up a bat, as he was due to lead off.

Chief grounded out, then took his usual seat on the bench next to Smoky. I put the bat back and joined them as Burns stepped into the batter's box.

"Did you get it?" Chief asked.

"It's there," Smoky said.

I was about to ask them what they were talking about when the crack of the bat and the roar of the crowd drew my eye to the field. Burns had ripped one up the alley in left center, and he was off and running.

I raced to the steps of the dugout to watch as Burns flew around second. The center fielder scooped up the ball and cut loose. Burns streaked toward third as the ball ate up the distance between them. Burns slid into the bag a hair before the Brooklyn third sacker could slap a tag on his leg.

I retrieved the bat and wished Pep Youngs good luck as he walked to the plate. Soon as I hit the dugout,

McGraw called me over. I lifted my cap, and he rubbed my head. Pep bunted the first pitch toward third. Grimes charged and threw home—too late to get the sliding Burns. The Giants led 1–0.

That single run opened the floodgates. Before I knew it, the Giants had five runs and Chief was due in the on-deck circle.

When Frisch came out instead, I turned and looked. There was an empty space next to Smoky on the bench. Chief was nowhere to be seen.

Grimes finally got out of the inning. I straightened the bats and slid onto the bench next to Smoky. Benton took over on the mound.

"Where's Chief?" I asked.

"He felt a twinge in his arm, so I asked McGraw to take him out."

"I think I'll duck into the locker room for a minute and see how he's doing," I said.

Smoky grabbed my wrist. "Stay here, Kernel Hank, and watch the game."

Bald No More

s you have probably guessed, that was the last I saw of Chief Sunrise. McGraw told the reporters that Chief had heard something snap in his arm and insisted on going back to the swamps of Florida to treat it with an old Seminole remedy. They looked like they didn't believe him, but not many people had the nerve to call McGraw a liar.

When I got back to our room—my room now—Chief's clothes were gone, and there was a note on my bed. I'd never seen Chief's writing. His letters were as gangly as his body. It said, "Hank, You were a great roomie. I hope someday we'll be teammates. Chief."

I was sitting on the bed, reading the note for maybe the hundredth time, when a knock came on the door. Before I could answer, John McGraw stepped in.

"We're going to miss him, Kernel," he said.

"Do you know where he's gone?" I asked, keeping my eyes on the note. I didn't want McGraw to think I was crying just because my eyes were watering from all the dust in that hotel.

"I don't, Hank," McGraw said, sitting next to me on the bed. "But I know it's somewhere with baseball. We'll watch for him in that new league next season."

It surprised me to hear McGraw say that, and my head popped up.

"Oh, I knew, Hank. Smoky spotted Chief for colored the first time he met you two. That's why I kept trying to get Chief to open up. I wanted him to confide in me."

"You let him pitch, knowing he's colored? Isn't that against the rules?"

McGraw sighed. He took a cigar from his pocket and reached for his matches. Then he seemed to think better of it and put the cigar in his mouth unlit.

"Kernel Hank, you can read every rule book there is, and you won't find a single rule against using colored players. The owners know that it's wrong to exclude Negroes. Otherwise, they'd put it in writing."

"Chief's the first colored I ever got to know," I said. "If they're all like him, I don't see why people hate them so."

"Ignorance and fear, Hank. There's good and bad in all colors." McGraw sighed. "Take Chase, for example. He doesn't think we can catch the Reds, so that gives him permission to sell out to the gamblers."

"You mean he dropped that throw on purpose?"

"I can't prove it, but you know Chief thought so. He shamed him by running that play over to first himself." McGraw laughed. "That was the best part of the game."

"What happens to me now?" I asked.

"Hank, you've been earning a small salary that I've been putting in the bank. Chief insisted on picking up your expenses."

Would I ever have a friend like that again? "I don't mean money," I said. "The season's almost over."

"Tomorrow my missus is coming to the game. We'll go out to dinner after, the three of us. We're hoping you'll live in our apartment in Graham Court once the season's over."

I felt like I had been buried under a pile of cypress logs, and McGraw had set me free.

"Thanks, Mr. McGraw."

"There's a catch, though, Hank. You'll have to go to school. That's why I'm relieving you of your duties as good-luck charm. Start letting your hair grow back so you can fit in with the other kids."

"How about my old man?" It seemed that whenever I was feeling good, he came into my mind and ruined it.

"Hank, the warden has pulled him off the prison ball club and taken away his privileges. He won't be talking to anyone for a while. If he decides to tell on Chief, it will be months before he gets the opportunity. By then Chief will have disappeared. There will be no proof."

"Will the gamblers be after Chief? He double-crossed them."

"I don't think your dad had time to tip off any gamblers, Hank. This was sort of a test run. If he saw he had Chief under control, he'd have set something up for the future."

Mr. McGraw squeezed my shoulder and left the room. I lay down on the bed to think. It sure was a crazy world. A war had just ended, yet people felt the need to fight with each other. Coloreds didn't enjoy the freedom to play on a team with whites, unless they were in prison.

And what would school be like? I'd never gone for more than a week or two in the past without the old man growing restless and pulling me out. Would I be able to take staying in one place, or did I have the wandering bug for good?

Then I thought of something that made me feel better. I pulled my glove from my shirt and worked my baseball deep into the pocket. I bet that school will have a baseball team.

Author's Note

J ohn McGraw is a member of the Baseball Hall of Fame. He was a star third baseman for the Baltimore Orioles of the late nineteenth century, then became even more famous as manager and part owner of the New York Giants. His feisty attitude earned him the hatred of opposing players, umpires, and anyone on his own team who didn't share his relentless desire to win.

McGraw was as superstitious in real life as he is in this novel. He believed bald heads were lucky. Crossed bats or crossed eyes were certain to put a jinx on a player or a whole team.

In 1919, McGraw signed the slick-fielding Hal Chase to be his first baseman, despite rumors that Chase was a less than honest player. Chase seemed to hit the ball hard and make great plays when the outcome of a game was no longer in doubt. At crucial moments, he made errors. Perhaps because of his own fierce desire to win, McGraw could not believe that anyone would deliberately lose a baseball game.

Near the end of the season, National League President John Heydler banned Hal Chase from baseball. A group of gamblers had testified that Chase had bet against his own team when he played for the Cincinnati Reds.

That Chase was not the only dirty player soon came to light. The Reds upset the heavily favored Chicago White Sox in the 1919 World Series. A few months later, it was learned that the World Series had been fixed. Eight of the White Sox players, including the magnificent hitter, Shoeless Joe Jackson, were banned from baseball for life. Hal Chase had brought the players and the gamblers together.

In an age when racial prejudice was taken for granted, John McGraw was color blind. He hired Smoky as his trainer and spent more time with him than with anyone else on the Giants. When he saw a chance to improve his team, McGraw didn't care if a player was black, white, or striped. Chief Sunrise is a fictional character. But, in 1901, John McGraw tried to sneak a black player onto his roster by pretending that he was a Native American.

McGraw, then the manager of the Baltimore Orioles, was staying at a hotel in Hot Springs, Arkansas. He happened to see the black bellhops playing baseball on the grounds. A young Negro named Charlie Grant so impressed McGraw that he decided to make him an Oriole. But McGraw knew that other teams would refuse to play against a Negro, and his own players might object as well.

His solution was to claim that Grant was a Native American. A map of the United States hung in the hotel lobby. McGraw noticed a place called Lake Tokohoma. He introduced Charlie Grant to everyone as Chief Tokohoma, a full-blooded Cherokee Indian.

Chief Tokohoma moved into the starting lineup at second base. He performed brilliantly as the Orioles played a series of exhibition games in preparation for the new season. But word of Charlie's true identity spread through the black community. Soon hordes of Negro fans were showing up for Orioles games. They cheered Charlie's every move on the diamond.

Reporters figured out McGraw's scam. When they threatened to print the story in their newspapers, McGraw sent Grant on his way. Charles Grant, playing under his own name, became one of the great stars of the Negro Leagues.

In 1916, a player named Jimmy Claxton got as far as the Oakland team of the Pacific Coast League, only one step below the majors. He, too, claimed to be a Native American. When it was discovered that he was a Negro, he was released. Not until 1947 did Jackie Robinson break the color line as a member of the Brooklyn Dodgers.

Sing Sing Prison did have a baseball team, although the warden didn't recruit players from other prisons as he does in my story. The Robins, Yankees, Giants, and

Phillies all visited the Ossining, New York, prison to play against the inmates.

There were indeed "Traveling Bloomers"—teams made up of girls, and young boys pretending to be girls. In their youth, future Hall of Famers Smoky Joe Wood and Rogers Hornsby played for Bloomers teams. I hope their experiences were less chaotic than Hank Cobb's.